D0114458

—The—
Betrayer's
Fortune

Trailblazer Books

Also by Dave and Neta Jackson

Hero Tales: A Family Treasury of True Stories
From the Lives of Christian Heroes (Volumes I, II, & III)

*Curriculum guide available.
Written by Julia Pferdehirt with Dave & Neta Jackson.   00B

—The—
Betrayer's
Fortune

DAVE & NETA JACKSON

Story Illustrations by
Julian Jackson

BETHANY HOUSE PUBLISHERS
MINNEAPOLIS, MINNESOTA 55438

Betrayer's Fortune
Copyright © 1994
Dave and Neta Jackson

Illustrations © 1994
Bethany House Publishers

Story illustrations by Julian Jackson.
Cover design and illustration by Catherine Reishus McLaughlin.

Published by Bethany House Publishers
A Ministry of Bethany Fellowship International
11400 Hampshire Avenue South
Minneapolis, Minnesota 55438
www.bethanyhouse.com

Printed in the United States of America by
Bethany Press International, Minneapolis, Minnesota 55438

Library of Congress Cataloging-in-Publication Data

Jackson, Dave
    The betrayer's fortune / Dave and Neta Jackson ; text illustrations by Julian Jackson.
        p.   cm. — (Trailblazer books ; #14)
    Summary: In Antwerp, Belgium, in 1543, after his mother is arrested as a heretic, fifteen-year-old Adriaen Wens flees with the Anabaptist preacher Menno Simons and must decide whether to turn Simons in to save his mother from death.

    1. Simons, Menno, 1496–1561—Juvenile fiction. [1. Simons, Menno, 1496–1561—Fiction. 2. Anabaptists—Fiction. 3. Mennonites—Fiction. 4. Christian life—Fiction.] I. Jackson, Neta. II. Jackson, Julian, ill. III. Title. IV. Series.
PZ7.J132418Be   1994
[Fic]—dc20   94–32700
ISBN 1–55661–467–5   CIP
                                                              AC

This story is set in 1543 when there was a price on Menno Simons' head. However, it merges three separate incidents that actually occurred later. Dirk Willems rescued his captor from the icy waters in 1569. The execution of Maeyken Wens and the letters to her son Adriaen happened in 1573. Hadewijk's humanly unexplainable release from prison happened in 1549. All these events (with the exception of Adriaen's involvement with Menno Simons) are true and represent typical experiences of the early Anabaptists, who considered themselves followers of Menno Simons, or "Mennonites." Although Menno Simons was said to have stayed in Hadewijk's "inn," Menno himself probably had no other contact with the other characters in this story.

Find us on the Web at . . .

trailblazerbooks.com

Meet the authors.

Read the first chapter of each book—with the pictures.

Track the Trailblazers around the world on a map.

Use the historical timeline to find out what other important events were happening in the world at the time of each Trailblazer story.

Discover how the authors research their books and link to some of the same sources they used where you can learn more about these heroes.

Write to the authors.

Explore frequently asked questions about the Trailblazer books and being writers.

Just point your browser to http://www.trailblazerbooks.com

CONTENTS

Chapter 1

The Merciful Outlaw

ADRIAEN WENS WAS TIRED of hauling sand for his father. He had been hauling sand and mixing mortar all day for three days, and his back felt as if it were breaking.

"We gotta take work where we can find it," his father insisted when Adriaen complained about having to work in Asperen, Holland—sixty miles north of their home in Antwerp, Belgium—even though everyone said the winter of 1543 was the harshest they could remember in a long time.

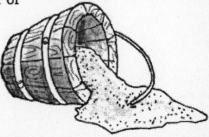

But a wealthy merchant in Asperen had heard of Mattheus

Wens's skill as a stonemason and hired him to build a new fireplace. "We should thank God for any work we can get," Mattheus chided his son. "Otherwise we couldn't even afford to put turnips on our table. Then where would Mother and the little ones be? Buck up now; we'll be goin' home soon . . . if you'll hustle and fetch me some more sand."

Just outside of Asperen, his father had found a pit with clean sand, perfect for mixing the mortar that would hold the stones together. "It's not easy to find clean sand in this marshy region," his father had said. "And if it's dirty, the mortar will crumble. So watch what you're doing. I don't want you bringin' me mud."

Adriaen pulled his hat lower and hoisted the yoke onto his muscled shoulders. Though he was small, he was strong for a boy of fifteen, but the wooden buckets that hung from each end of the yoke were heavy even when empty. He slammed the heavy wooden door closed with a *thump* and headed down the narrow cobblestoned street toward the edge of town. He didn't bother to turn as he heard a loud commotion behind him. But suddenly someone hit the left arm of his yoke, spinning him around and almost knocking him down.

"Sorry, friend," a kid about his own age called as he dashed past Adriaen. "Whatcha doin' with those buckets? Come on with us . . . this should be fun!"

"Where ya goin'?" Adriaen called, but the boy was gone, pushed along by a crowd of excited people pouring down the street like flood waters through a broken dike. Adriaen caught the sleeve of another passerby. "What's happenin'?"

"The fox has escaped, but the thiefcatcher's hot on his trail!" said the man, pulling away. Adriaen was buffeted along as people hit the yoke across his shoulders. The crowd had become a real mob. If he wasn't careful, he could trip and be trampled.

Suddenly, a narrow walkway opened up between two buildings. Adriaen dropped his sand buckets and yoke into the opening, and joined the crowd at a trot. The people acted as if they were going to a circus. He caught snatches of excited talk:

"That chap was fast . . ."

"Gone like a rabbit. Dodged right under that thiefcatcher's arm . . ."

"If the thiefcatcher would lose a little weight, he could've had him—heh, heh—but . . ."

At the edge of town the cobblestoned street turned into a dirt road of frozen ruts, and the tightly packed buildings gave way to scattered shacks with small gardens around them. Then the crowd surged past farmland dotted with isolated houses, barns, and windmills across the open fields. The frosty ground was hard with yellow stubble sticking above a dusting of snow.

Adriaen ran to get to the head of the slowing crowd. As he pushed to the front Adriaen could see two figures—one behind the other—jogging along a short ways ahead.

"He's got him now," wheezed a red-faced man who walked a few steps and then trotted a little to catch up. "They're headin' right for the canal with no bridge for miles either way."

"What'd he steal?" asked Adriaen.

"Ha! Prob'ly nothin' more than a crust o' bread, but he sure gave Hartog the slip—dodgin' this way and that all around the town square whenever Hartog made a grab for him. The burgomaster was so mad, he threatened to hire a new thiefcatcher and lock ol' Hartog in the stocks!" The man wheezed a short laugh. "I *told* Hartog that he spends too much time with a mug of beer in his face, but he wouldn't listen to me. Now . . . ha! He finds out he's not so fast as he used to be."

Adriaen glanced at the man's red face and watery eyes and noted how hard he puffed as they hurried along. The man probably knew from experience how much Hartog drank . . . the experience of keeping up with him, mug for mug.

The crowd arrived at the bank of the canal in time to see the fugitive scamper gingerly out onto the slick ice while the thiefcatcher stood on the bank yelling threats at him.

"Come on, Hartog! Go get him!" yelled someone.

"Yeah, what's keepin' ya?"

Dark water could be seen through the smooth surface of the ice. Anyone could tell that the ice wasn't very thick. The fugitive was wiry and light; the thiefcatcher was stout.

Hartog tested his footing; the ice held. He took another step.

"After him, man! He's getting away. Let's see you

earn your bread for a change," someone in the crowd heckled.

"Yeah, and your beer, too," added the red-faced man, causing the whole crowd to roar with laughter.

The fugitive was almost to the other bank when the thiefcatcher decided to go for it. Taking little steps as though he were barefoot and didn't want his toes to freeze, he danced out onto the ice. Suddenly the surface began to pop and snap as if someone were cracking a whip. Lines in the ice spread from under Hartog's boots. He scampered faster with his arms outstretched to keep his balance, but water was oozing up through the cracks.

The fugitive reached the bank.

Hartog was only a few yards from safety when, with a cry, more cracking, and a great whoosh, he dropped through the ice. His arms slapped wildly, churning the dark water into a white foam, but he sank lower and lower.

The crowd was screaming advice: "Swim for it!" "Grab the edge, man!"

Then the thiefcatcher went under, and everyone fell silent.

He surfaced coughing and choking. "Help!" he managed to gasp as he turned toward the bank where his fellow citizens stood helplessly watching. "Somebody help me!"

No one moved.

"Please, somebody!" pleaded Hartog. "Help me!"

But everybody knew that, with the ice so thin and already cracked from Hartog's attempted crossing, it would have been suicide to follow him.

Adriaen noticed that the fugitive had stopped running. He stood looking back a moment, then started running again just as Hartog's cries for help were choked off by the frigid water.

The outlaw glanced back over his shoulder as the thiefcatcher's body sank below the surface of the black water. He stopped running, turned, and started walking back along the opposite canal bank, watching the hole in the ice. His steps got faster and faster, and when the thiefcatcher didn't bob quickly to the surface, he broke into a run.

Just as the man arrived at the point where he had climbed the bank, the waters began to stir again, and Hartog's head slowly broke the surface, water streaming down his anguished face. He coughed and tried to yell something, but he was too weak to keep fighting.

The fugitive looked across the canal at the crowd; then he ripped off his coat and scrambled down the bank. At the edge of the ice, he fell onto his stomach and slid out on the ice, crawling with his arms and legs to scoot forward.

When he was within reach, he threw his coat out ahead of him into the hole of icy water where the drowning man could grasp it. But Hartog was too far gone to realize that help was at hand. The fugitive yelled at him, pulled his coat back, and cast it out again so that it slapped the water just behind the thiefcatcher's head.

But it was no good; the man was slowly slipping

under. With one motion, the fugitive slid forward a
few more feet until his face was over the open water,

and then he reached out and grasped the hair of the drowning man.

He pulled him to the edge of the ice, then scooted himself back. He tried to pull the man up onto the ice, but the angle was wrong and the man was too heavy. Finally, the outlaw took the risk of standing up on the ice so he could lift the man.

The edge of the ice began to break, but the fugitive kept his hold as he shuffled backward and was able to pull the man's head and shoulders out of the water. Little by little, he got the man's heavy body up onto the ice. The thiefcatcher began to revive. Coughing and sputtering, he was able to pull his legs out of the water, and with the help of the fugitive, he began to crawl.

Together they made it safely to the bank as a great cheer went up from the crowd across the canal. When the two men were both safely standing on the shore, the fugitive put his coat around the shoulders of the freezing man as the man clung to him.

On the other side of the canal, a carriage pulled to a stop behind the onlookers, and a very fat, fancily dressed man stepped out. Seeing the crowd open a path as the man made his way to the edge of the canal, Adriaen figured that he must be the town mayor—known in those parts as the *burgomaster*.

"Good work, thiefcatcher!" the burgomaster yelled across the canal. "Keep a tight hold on that man. We don't want him getting away again."

The crowd booed loudly, and the thiefcatcher yelled back, "But he just saved my life. Why should I hold him? He pulled me from the canal!"

"Let him go!" came cries from the crowd.

"Yeah, give the man a break," others joined in with a supportive cheer.

The burgomaster turned his great body toward the people, his face stern and frowning. "We don't conduct justice by giving people 'breaks,'" he said loudly enough for all to hear. Then he turned back toward the canal and yelled, "Don't you *dare* let go of that man, Hartog. I want him brought in now!"

There was no doubt that the thiefcatcher *was* holding on to the fugitive, but it was more to hold himself up as he shivered than to prevent the man from escaping. "Please, sir," he called back. "I'm nearly frozen, and the man saved my life. He could have easily gotten away . . . but he came back to help me."

"Let him go!" rose the cries from the crowd again.

"You hold him fast," bellowed the burgomaster. "His coming back to rescue you just shows what fools these heretics are."

"Heretic?" As the word was whispered through the crowd, the mood suddenly changed. "Let him burn," someone muttered, and soon others picked up the call. "Let him burn! . . . Let him burn!"

Adriaen was astonished. The same people who had just appealed for the man's release a few minutes ago were now shouting for his death. They acted like a circus crowd demanding more "entertainment." "To the stake!" they cried.

"But I'm shaking so bad with cold . . . I don't think

I can walk, sir," protested the thiefcatcher from across the canal, clutching his prey.

"Don't worry, Hartog!" yelled the red-faced man who was still near Adriaen. "You'll soon be able to warm yourself with the same fire that cooks your man."

The mob roared with laughter.

"You keep a tight hold on him, or I'll have you executed in his place. *Then* you'll know what warm is," threatened the burgomaster. "Now . . . head west along the canal toward Walen's Crossing. I'll drive my carriage down that way and meet you at the bridge. Understood?"

With that, the burgomaster climbed back into his carriage, and with a snap of the driver's whip, the horses wheeled back the way they had come.

Chapter 2

Mama's Gone!

ONCE THE BURGOMASTER had driven off in his carriage, the crowd drifted back toward town, chattering eagerly about the additional excitement they expected to come later that day. A burning!

Adriaen followed along, his hands jammed in his pockets and his head down. He didn't like what had happened at the canal.

Why was that man being condemned to death? What had he done that was so wrong? He couldn't be such an evil man or he never would have come back to rescue the thiefcatcher. But . . . why had the burgomaster called him a heretic?

Adriaen knew that the ac-

cusation of "heretic" could mean many things. It supposedly referred to an evil person who didn't believe Christian truth and tried to confuse other people with false teachings. But . . . the accusation was sometimes made against anyone who didn't go along with the beliefs of the official state church.

The boy glanced around at the crowd uneasily. His own family was part of a small "house church" back in Antwerp. Because it was not part of the official state church, its members were often called heretics. In fact, a few years earlier there had been a bad persecution of the "believers," as they were called, and several were arrested and sent to prison and tortured; a few were even put to death.

After that, the believers met secretly in people's homes. Adriaen had been told there were many such secret churches all over Europe. His parents, and most of the believers in that part of Europe, followed the teachings of a man named Menno Simons, so they were sometimes called "Mennonists" or "Mennonites." Simons had once been a priest in the Roman Catholic Church . . . until he began reading the Bible for himself. Then he discovered that many of the teachings of the state church were wrong.

Coarse laughter interrupted Adriaen's thoughts, and the uneasy feeling returned. He doubted that the man who had been "captured" at the canal deserved death . . . but he was most upset by the way the crowd had suddenly turned into an ugly mob. One minute the people were chasing the poor fellow for sport . . . then they cheered him for rescuing

Hartog . . . only to switch to calling for his death at the word "heretic."

It was scary.

A cold wind stung Adriaen's cheeks and blew away his frosty breath. Something else troubled him about the whole incident. He felt guilty . . . but he didn't know why. *He* hadn't cheered when the mob called for the fugitive to be burned at the stake. So why did he feel as though he had been a part of the whole mess?

Adriaen was almost back to town when he remembered that his father was expecting him to bring sand. *Oh, no! Papa's going to be very angry at having to wait.* Adriaen decided he must be feeling guilty because he hadn't done what his father had told him. Quickly he ran back into town, found his sand buckets where he'd dumped them, and hurried to the sand pit. Working feverishly, he filled the buckets in record time.

✧ ✧ ✧ ✧

"So what took you so long?" asked Mattheus when Adriaen came puffing into the house. "I've been waiting for more sand. If we don't get this job done today, we're going to have to stay over another day. I thought you were the one who wanted to get home."

Adriaen remained silent as he dumped the sand from his buckets and quickly began mixing the mortar. But his father was not satisfied. "I asked what took you so long?"

21

"I got delayed," murmured Adriaen, hoping that would satisfy his father.

"Huh! You weren't delayed digging sand. I went out there to check and you weren't even there. So . . . where were you?"

Adriaen gave up. He might as well tell the whole story. He finished by saying, "I—I'm really sorry, Father. On my way back I was feeling guilty, and then I realized it was because you'd be waiting for the sand."

Mattheus frowned and rubbed his chin thoughtfully. "Yes. Well, there's no doubt that I was getting rather upset at having to wait for the sand. But . . . I suspect that wasn't the only thing that made you feel guilty."

"Whaddya mean? I didn't do anything else," Adriaen said defensively.

"I'm not condemning you, son, but you just told me how ugly that mob got, and yet you were there with the lot of them. You, too, ran out there to watch some poor soul get chased down."

"But . . . I didn't mean any harm."

"Of course not. We never do. Sin always starts with something small—like finding amusement in someone else's misfortune. The thing that scared you was realizing how close you came to taking part in their bloodthirst." Mattheus bent down and sorted through the final stones for the hearth as the boy continued mixing the mortar. "That's a very mature thing to see, son. Most adults don't understand Jesus' truth when He said, 'He that is faithful in that which is least is faithful also in much: and he that is unjust in the least is unjust also in much.' "

The boy thought for a moment. "You're right, Papa. I guess just being there made me feel guilty."

"Well, the Lord forgives you. Just remember, when someone else is being abused, if we are not part of the solution, then we are part of the problem. That's just the way the human family works. We *are* our brother's keeper."

Adriaen took the batch of mortar to his father, and they worked together in silence for a while until his father said, "Say, what did that fellow look like?"

"You mean the fugitive? He was a thin sort of man—but wiry and strong. He managed to pull that big thiefcatcher out of the water. I don't know . . . he was all the way across the canal."

"Still, think on it. What'd he look like?"

"Well . . . he had a pointed chin with a little red beard on the end, and a very sharp nose."

"Was he wearing a blue, threadbare coat with some ragged fur around the collar—like it was a castoff from someone else?"

"Why . . . yes. As a matter of fact, that's what he flung into the water for the thiefcatcher to grab. I remember when he tried to put it on after they were out of the water, it didn't come near fitting. But . . . how did you know?"

"Because that man's no more a heretic than I am, Adriaen. His name is Dirk Willems, and he's one of our own brethren. I met him three days ago."

Suddenly Adriaen's mouth felt very dry. "Do you

think the persecution is starting up again?" he asked quietly.

"Possibly. I've heard that the emperor is again trying to stamp out the church reformers—especially the 'Anabaptists,' which is what they call those of us who insist on being rebaptized as believers. I heard they're making another effort to capture Menno Simons." Mattheus sighed. "I'll sure be glad to get out of this town and back with the family. We're not part of the church here, so we wouldn't know who to trust if we needed help. And being strangers, we automatically call attention to ourselves."

It was well after dark that night before they finished. The master of the house didn't like having to inspect their work so late. "Why can't this wait until morning?" he grumbled as he rubbed his hands over the cold stones.

"Well, sir," said Mattheus, "we were hoping to get a start for home before first light in the morning—presuming our work meets with your approval—and we knew you wouldn't want to be wakened that early."

"Not on your life. But how do I know that this fireplace will draw properly and won't smoke up my whole room the first time I light it? I know we can't build a fire in it until the mortar cures proper."

"That's right. I wouldn't recommend a fire for at least three days. But watch this." The mason took a handful of straw, lit it with a candle, and held it into the mouth of the fireplace. "There . . . you see how the smoke goes right up? If it will draw cold, it will for sure draw proper when it's hot with a full blaze in it."

"Hmm," muttered the merchant. "I s'pose you're right. Well, then, here's your wages, and a good trip to you."

"Thank you . . . thank you, sir. And if there is ever anything else you need doing, all you have to do is send for me. Thank you very much."

"Well, I do need a garden wall—"

"Thank you. Maybe in the spring, but right now we need to be getting home to the family."

✧ ✧ ✧ ✧

Three nights later father and son trudged into their hometown of Antwerp, looking forward to one of Maeyken Wens's hearty, homecooked meals. Adriaen was eager to see his sisters and brother. Elsie was ten and helped Mama a lot around the kitchen. At age six, quiet little Levina had her chores, too. Mostly she looked after three-year-old Hans, who was always into mischief.

But when they turned into their alley, there were no lights in the small windows of their apartment above the butcher shop, and no smoke curled from the chimney.

They climbed the outside stairs with anxious hearts. "Hello . . . ! We're home," Adriaen's father announced as he opened the door, but no one responded. The room was cold. The cookstove was cold. No one had been there for some time.

They pounded on their neighbor's door, across the hall. At first no one came to the door, but they had seen a dim light in their neighbor's window when they arrived home, so they kept trying. "Hello! It's Mattheus. Do you know where Maeyken and the little ones are?"

Finally, they heard shuffling inside, and a woman's hushed voice came through the closed door: "Go away! Just go away."

"But what has happened? Where is my wife?" Mattheus demanded.

"I don't know. I don't know anything about them. Just go away." The shuffling died away and the light under the door went out.

"Where could they be?" asked Adriaen anxiously, following his father back down the stairs. They looked around the gloomy alley, not knowing what they might find but hoping for some clue concerning the whereabouts of their family.

Mattheus said, "I'm getting worried, Adriaen. Maeyken would have left some kind of word if she could, knowing we'd be home soon. Something's not right."

"We could go over to the Metsers," Adriaen suggested. "They might know where Mother is."

"Possibly . . . and I suppose you wouldn't mind seeing Betty either, would you?" teased his father, trying to lighten their spirits a little.

Adriaen flushed. Betty was an orphan about his own age living with the Metsers, a family who also worshiped in their secret church. Her mother had died when Betty was born, and she didn't know who her father was. For a while she lived with one aunt, then another, but when she was about ten, her relatives could no longer be "bothered," so the girl was kicked out into the streets. The Metsers had found her nearly starved and took her in. In their home she had learned about Jesus, had become a devout believer and—to Adriaen's surprise—had already been "rebaptized," just like his own parents.

His family teased Adriaen about Betty. He hotly denied being interested in her, but sometimes—when he was alone—he admitted to himself that he kind of liked her . . . a little, maybe.

Besides, as he and his father walked quickly to the Metsers', his spirits lifted a little to have some place to go, someone to turn to. If there was trouble, they would need friends, and there were none more true and trustworthy than their fellow believers.

In answer to Mattheus Wens's knock, John Metser hurriedly motioned them in. Then he looked up and down the street before quickly closing the door.

"Papa!"

A wild yell came from the next room, and Hans, Adriaen's little brother, ran across the small room and leaped into his father's arms, followed by his two sisters, Elsie and Levina, who smothered Mattheus and Adriaen with hugs and kisses.

"We were worried about you!" Adriaen said to his sisters, untangling himself. "Why weren't you home? And where's Mama?"

"It's a long story," spoke up John Metser hastily, glancing out the one small window in the front of the house. "But first . . . sit yourselves down at the table here and get some nourishment in you. You've had a long journey."

Mrs. Metser, a round, motherly woman, dished up some still-hot soup from a big pot on the stove, and Betty, her long, honey-colored hair peeking out from under her cap, shyly served it with bread to Adriaen and his father. The younger Wens children stood around their father and brother as they began to eat.

Again, John Metser cautiously drew the window curtain back and looked out.

"You're as nervous as a caged cat, John," said Mattheus, frowning, as he tore off a hunk of bread and stuffed it into his mouth. "Are you expecting someone? What about Maeyken . . . will she be coming soon to pick up the children? Where did she go, anyway? We were worried when we got home and no one was there!"

"Well," said John, dropping the curtain, "I want to make sure you weren't followed, Mattheus. As for Maeyken" —the man looked sadly at his two visitors— "the reason she isn't here is because . . ." He paused, struggling for words.

"Yes, yes—go on, man!" said Mattheus, looking at his friend anxiously.

John Metser took a big breath. "Your wife . . . she's been arrested."

Chapter 3

Arrested

"Arrested!" Mattheus Wens blurted in shock. "But ... how? Why?"

Slowly the story came out: Maeyken Wens and two other women had gone to the Munstdorps' home for a prayer meeting, when soldiers had forced their way in and arrested all five believers. They were being held in the Antwerp prison, and city officials were looking for any relatives or friends of the believers in hopes of smashing the small underground church in Antwerp.

Adriaen just stared at the bowl of soup getting cold in front of him. Mama in prison? It couldn't be! Not his kind and gentle mother!

"As soon as we discovered what had happened, we went over and got your children and brought them here . . . that was yesterday morning," spoke up Mrs. Metser gently.

"Bless you, friends," said Mattheus, speaking with difficulty. "Do . . . the officials know where we live or who we are?"

"I don't think so," said John. "Your neighbor woman across the hall may be suspicious. She wanted to know why I was taking the children and started to make an awful fuss until one of your girls spoke up and assured her that they knew us well. Can you trust her?"

"Only God knows," sighed Mattheus, pulling at the short beard on his chin. "She's a good woman, but I don't know what she thinks about us Anabaptists. Tonight she wouldn't even open her door to me. She just kept saying, 'Go away. Go away!' "

"Then she's scared about something," said Mrs. Metser. "Maybe I can talk to her tomorrow and test out whether she is safe with our secret."

"Thank you, Sister Metser . . . that'll be good. And tomorrow I'll go visit Maeyken in prison," said Mattheus.

"No, no! You mustn't do that, Mattheus," John Metser warned, checking out the window one more time. "The authorities are searching everywhere and would be only too glad to identify you when you visited your wife."

"But . . . we can't just leave Mama in prison

without contacting her!" cried Adriaen. "She would come to us—no matter what the risk."

"But it's not just you at risk," reasoned Mrs. Metser. "If they discovered that Mattheus was her husband, it would endanger all the rest of us. We can't let that happen. The safety of the whole church must be considered."

"But . . . how would you feel if you were in prison and no one came to visit you? You just can't do it!" Suddenly Adriaen was angry. It just wasn't fair. Then he remembered something . . .

" 'I was in prison, and ye came unto me,' " he blurted, quoting a verse from the Bible. "Jesus said that those people would inherit the kingdom. But the other people He sent to hell and said, 'I was in prison, and ye visited me not.' I remember those verses. You preached on them yourself, Mr. Metser. So we can't just leave her there alone!"

Everyone was silent. Finally, with a pained look on her face Mrs. Metser said, "I know, son. It's terrible not being able to visit her, but—"

"Maybe the best we can do," offered Betty, "is pray."

"*Pray?* Pray for what? That's easy for you to say," said Adriaen bitterly. "Your mama's not in that terrible prison—" He stopped in shock as he remembered that she didn't even have a mother.

Some time later the small family of father, older son, and three young children walked quietly through the streets of Antwerp on their way back to their own home. They kept to the shadows, peeking around corners before venturing down a street. It all seemed to be going well when suddenly a man stepped out of a doorway. "Hold up there," he ordered, blocking their path.

"Please step aside, friend," said Mattheus pleasantly.

The figure grabbed Father's shoulder. "Not 'til you tell me what I need to know."

Adriaen was terrified. Should he take the girls and run? Should he try to distract the man so his father could get away? What if there were others waiting to arrest them all?

But his father didn't seemed concerned. "What do you need to know?" he asked calmly.

"Need to know . . . need to know which way George went. Have you seen 'im? 'E took our jug of wine. We're s'posed ta be buddies . . . s'posed ta share. But when I woke up, he was gone. So I need to know: Which way did he go. . . ?" The man lurched to one side.

Adriaen sighed with relief. The man was not a thiefcatcher or city official . . . just a confused drunk.

"I'm sorry," said Mattheus, "we don't know anyone named George. But if you need a place to stay for the night, you can come to our house. We're headed there now."

"Thanks anyway, but . . . say, have you seen George? I need to find him—" and the man staggered off into the night as the family hurried on to their home.

Adriaen slept badly. It wasn't just that the house and his bed were cold; it was that every time he rolled over, he woke up with the horrible feeling that something terrible had happened. At first he wasn't able to remember what it was. Then suddenly the realization would slam into him: *Mama was in prison!* Everything was so wrong. He tossed and turned as the words tumbled through his mind again and again: "I was in prison, and ye visited me not . . . I was in prison, and ye visited me not." Finally, after what seemed like hours, he would drift back into a dream-filled, troubled sleep.

When morning finally arrived, Adriaen felt like crying. Why had this happened? Had he done something wrong? Was God punishing him by taking his mother away? He searched his memory, remembering the times he'd been mean to his sisters and brother, the times when he hadn't obeyed his parents as he should have.

Then . . . he remembered how he'd followed the crowd out of town in Asperen to watch the thiefcatcher chase Dirk Willems. *That must be it,* he thought, remembering how his father had chided him for going along. *God must be angry with me . . . He's punishing me for following the thiefcatcher.* But the thought had no sooner entered his mind than Adriaen felt his chest tighten with his own anger. *If God sent Mama to prison because I followed the thiefcatcher, then . . . He's a mean God, He's not fair! Why should Mama pay for something I did?* At the same time Adriaen felt terribly guilty.

That morning Mattheus left to find work as usual. "I'll see if I can get hired to work on that new bridge," he told Adriaen. "It doesn't pay as well as private jobs, but if the authorities haven't identified us yet, then life must go on as usual. Steady work in a public place would arouse the least suspicion."

Adriaen was dumbfounded. *Go to work? How can life go on as usual with Mama in prison?* He looked away from his father.

That day Mattheus did get hired to work on the bridge. But the days that followed were long and hard; each night when he got home he anxiously asked if there had been any news from Maeyken. But there was none.

While his father was at work, Adriaen took care of his sisters and brother . . . but it was hard when Hans cried himself to sleep at nap time because Mama wasn't there. The girls tried hard, but the housework and cooking always seemed to end in some kind of mess. And then there were the long nights, waking in the dark, struggling with the feeling that something was terribly wrong . . .

Adriaen was almost glad to escape the family flat each day to empty the slop water and refill his water buckets at the town fountain. Not knowing what was happening to his mother felt like an open sore on his heart . . . and besides, he couldn't get the words of Jesus out of his mind: "I was in prison, and ye visited me not." *Someone* had to visit his mother.

Slowly an idea grew in Adriaen's mind. *Maybe visiting Mama in prison is a way to obey Jesus,* he thought. *And if no one else will visit her, maybe I should. No one would suspect a boy of being a member of the secret church.*

Technically that was true. The Anabaptists believed that a person had to be old enough to make an "adult decision" to become a member of the church. They did not baptize babies into the church as the state church did. "Baptizing an infant mocks the ordinance of baptism," Menno Simons taught his followers. "How can a baby understand that he is a sinner and choose to repent and give his life to Christ? You have to be old enough to know what you are doing for baptism to have any true meaning."

But Adriaen was old enough to make a decision for himself. Betty had. She had been baptized the previous fall. Since then Adriaen often thought about becoming a Jesus-follower, too. Because he had been raised in a home where the Bible was taught, Adriaen usually wanted to do what Jesus said, even though he had not yet been baptized. But sometimes he didn't know what he wanted to do.

Now was one of those times. *Why should I give my life to a God who would allow my innocent mother to be sent to prison?* he muttered to himself as he trudged back to the flat with the heavy water buckets.

And if he were honest with himself, Adriaen would have had to admit that what mattered most at that point was not what God wanted him to do but simply his desire to visit his mother. Somebody had to visit her—and if no one else was going to go to the prison, he would go visit her himself!

Chapter 4

Under Lock and Key

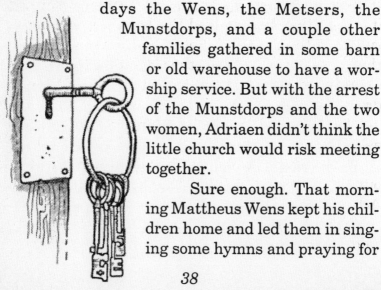

T HE NEXT DAY WAS SUNDAY, so Adriaen had no chance to go visit his mother. Usually on Sundays the Wens, the Metsers, the Munstdorps, and a couple other families gathered in some barn or old warehouse to have a worship service. But with the arrest of the Munstdorps and the two women, Adriaen didn't think the little church would risk meeting together.

Sure enough. That morning Mattheus Wens kept his children home and led them in singing some hymns and praying for their mother. Then he said, "There's a Bible story I want to tell you. It comes from Acts twelve. The apostle Peter had been arrested for preaching about Jesus, and the ruler Herod threw him into prison, but the church prayed hard for him."

Adriaen frowned. Did his father have to tell them *this* story?

"The night before his trial," Mattheus went on, "Peter was sleeping, bound in chains between two soldiers. There were other guards at the prison doors as well. Suddenly an angel of the Lord appeared and a light shone in the cell and woke Peter up. 'Quick, get up!' said the angel, and the chains fell off Peter's wrists.

"Then the angel told him, 'Put on your clothes and sandals and follow me.' So Peter followed him out of the prison. They passed the first and second guards and came to the iron gate leading to the city. It opened for them by itself, and they went through it. When they had walked the length of one street, suddenly the angel left Peter, and Peter went on to the house of some of the other believers."

Mattheus stopped and looked at each of his children.

"Is the angel gonna let Mama out of prison?" asked Hans, his eyes wide.

"I don't know, child . . . I just don't know. But it's our job to keep praying like the church in the Book of Acts did."

"You're just getting their hopes up for nothin'," said Adriaen bitterly.

Mattheus looked sadly at his oldest son. "No, not for nothing. Besides, I'm not encouraging our hopes . . . but our faith. There's a difference."

"What difference?"

"We *hope* for a lot of things, and it's important to pray for those things. God tells us to bring our requests to Him, and He will hear us. We hope and pray for Mama's release . . . but God has not promised us *exactly* what will happen to Mama or how He will answer most of the personal things we ask for. How do we survive if something we hope for doesn't happen the way we wish?"

Good question, Adriaen thought.

"That's where faith comes in," his father said. "Faith is the confidence that God *is* there, that He loves us, hears our prayers, and is in control—no matter what happens."

"It sounds like you're saying that God might let Mama die even though we pray for her release. Why should we have faith in God if He lets something that bad happen to us?" Adriaen challenged.

"God has promised 'that all things work together for good to them that love God,'" Mattheus said gently. "What may seem bad to us now may be the most loving thing in the long run—it may later work together for good in ways we can't imagine right now. Faith that God loves us and is in control is sometimes the only thing that keeps us going."

At first, what his father said made sense to Adriaen . . . that is, until he thought about his mother. Then he felt there was only *one* good outcome: the release of his mother.

"Now," said Mattheus as he stood up, indicating that their worship time had come to an end, "it's almost time for us to go. Get your coats and bundle up. It's cold out today."

"Where are we going, Papa?" asked little Hans, running to get his coat.

"To meet with the other brothers and sisters."

"But I thought it was too dangerous to gather together today," said Elsie.

"Ah-ha. But I have a plan."

❖ ❖ ❖ ❖

In a short time the Wens family arrived at the riverfront. At that point the Schelde River was very wide as it moved slowly toward the sea. In fact, when the tide was high, salt water from the sea would surge up the river, so it was almost like being on a small bay. The port of Antwerp was an important shipping site for Belgium, and many large, seagoing ships rested at the docks.

At the end of a small pier they could see several people getting into a large, open boat. Suddenly, Adriaen realized that they were the members of their secret church. The Metsers were there, as well as several other people.

"Now, don't be greeting other people," Mattheus Wens said softly to his children as they got closer. "Just act like we are all strangers who happen to be getting into the same boat to cross over the Schelde."

"Where are we going?" demanded Adriaen, hanging back. If they were fleeing Antwerp, he wasn't going along. He wasn't going to leave his mother rotting in prison alone.

"Just come along, son, and don't make a scene."

"I'm not leavin' Mama!"

"Shh. We're not leaving her. Just trust me. Now come along and act normal."

Reluctantly, Adriaen walked out on the small dock and climbed into the boat. Curious, Adriaen counted heads . . . sixteen people found seats in the heavy boat, then three men on each side took up oars and slowly moved the vessel out onto the water. John Metser was at the back steering the rudder.

Once they were far enough out into the water so that people on the shore and the men working on the docks couldn't easily hear them, everyone began to relax and greet one another.

"Greetings, Sister Metser . . . you too, Betty."

"Mattheus! We're deeply sorry to hear about Maeyken . . ."

"Has anyone heard from the Munstdorps?"

So far there had been no news. On one hand, that was good news: The prisoners had not been executed outright. They would probably get a trial. But everyone was eager for some news.

As the oarsmen rowed farther down the river, it got wider and the cold breeze kicked up small waves. Between the light wind and the slap of the waves, there was no way people on shore could hear them. John Metser said, "This ought to do. Let's begin by

singing a song."

And in this way, the small group of Anabaptists

had a worship service on that cold Sunday morning.

✧ ✧ ✧ ✧

The next day after his father had gone to work, Adriaen quickly did his chores and made sure his sisters and brother would be safe. "I have to go on an errand," he told Elsie. "You watch out for Hans . . . and don't leave the house."

"Can I come with you?" Hans begged.

"No. You stay here with Levina and Elsie."

"But I wanna go!"

"You can't. Just stay here and do as they say."

"I bet you're going to see Betty," teased Elsie.

"No, I'm not," said Adriaen, reddening. "I just have to do something."

He stuffed some bread rolls that Mrs. Metser had given them into an old sack, threw on his coat, and clattered down the outside steps. It took an hour of hard walking to get to the prison, and once the huge stone walls loomed into view, he realized he did not know how to get in or whom to ask for permission to visit his mother.

He walked back and forth on the opposite side of the street from the prison until he saw a woman wearing a thin, patched coat coming out of the gate. Adriaen followed her for a block. "Excuse me, ma'am," he said, catching up with her. "Were you visiting someone in the prison?"

The woman turned to him; tears were streaming down her cheeks. Adriaen felt embarrassed for having bothered her. But before he could apologize, she said, "Yes. My husband. He's going to be hung a week from Friday."

"I . . . I'm sorry," Adriaen stammered. "I didn't know." He started to back away when she held up her hand.

"That's all right, son. What did you want?"

The boy felt awkward. "I—I need to get into the prison to see someone, but I don't know how."

"Do you have kinsfolk in there? They only let family members in."

"I do, but . . . I can't say who it is."

"Why not, boy? You gotta tell who you want to see. They're not gonna let you in there to wander around talking to everyone."

Adriaen hesitated, and then, after looking around, he said softly, "It's my mother, but I don't want them to know that I'm her son."

"Well, why not? You haven't done anything wrong, have you?"

"No. But . . . I've got my reasons. I can't tell them who I am."

Adriaen was so earnest that the woman finally shook her head and said, "All right, all right. I've been coming here for a long time, and I know some of the guards, especially the one right inside the gate. I'll say something to him, and see if he'll let you in. You come on along and just wait out of sight."

Adriaen was grateful but scared.

"What's her name?" the woman asked.

Adriaen hesitated. He didn't know this woman.

What if she betrayed him?

"Come on . . . there's no way you're going to see your mother if you don't tell me who she is. But you can trust me, boy . . . I'll try not to let on who you are."

Just as they got to the gate, Adriaen mumbled, "Maeyken . . . Maeyken Wens."

"What?"

"I *said*, Maeyken Wens."

"Maeyken Wens, huh? All right. You wait around the corner there . . . I'll see what I can do." She began rattling the gate and calling for a guard. "Gunter . . . Gunter!" she hollered. "Come back out here. I need to see you."

Finally, a man with a deep, raspy voice arrived and said, "What are you doin' back here, Emma? I thought you were already here today. Go on home. There's nothin' you can do for your man. He's gonna swing. I'm sorry for you . . . and him, too. But you can't stop it now."

Adriaen cringed and could see Emma drop her head. When she raised it again, she said, "It's not for me. I'm here for someone else."

"You got someone else in jail?"

"No, no . . . there's a boy here who wants to see someone. I told him I'd ask if you'd let him in."

"Hey, now . . . we don't open the gates to everyone who comes along," the guard barked. "You know that, Emma. Who is it, anyway?"

"Gunter," said Emma in frustration, "just let the kid in."

"I'm takin' a risk here, you know. What's in it for me?"

"Don't worry 'bout that. You know me. I'm not gonna report you, and the kid's sure not gonna say anything."

"Well, who's he want to see?"

"A woman named Maeyken Wens."

"Never heard of her. Maeyken who? What's she in for?"

"See, Gunter? You got too many people in there. You can't even keep track of them all. I don't know what she's in for. But believe me; she's in there, or the kid wouldn't be askin' to see her. Now just let him in!"

"Who is he? Why does he want to see her? He's gotta be kin to get in, ya know."

"Just let him in, will ya?"

"All right, all right . . . I'll let him in. But you know these gates; once they slam closed behind a person, they don't always open again." The man roared with laughter and turned a big key in the lock.

The woman waved for Adriaen to step out from around the corner. Adriaen hesitated. "Come on. Come on!" she said. "He's not gonna hold the gate open all day. You want in, or not?"

Adriaen stepped cautiously through the gate, and a huge man wearing a heavy leather coat slammed and locked it behind him. The guard didn't really have a beard, but his face looked as though he hadn't shaved for a week or more. He sneered down at

47

Adriaen. "Gotta check you for weapons and contra-band. Wouldn't want you smuggling anything illegal to the prisoners, now, would we?"

"I haven't got anything," protested Adriaen.

"That's for me to decide. What's in that bag?"

"Just some bread."

"Dump it out."

Adriaen opened the bag and held it out for the man to inspect.

"I said dump it!" And he grabbed the sack out of Adriaen's hands and turned it upside down, scattering the rolls all over the ground. "Give me your coat."

That time Adriaen obeyed immediately. The man felt all through the coat to make sure nothing was hidden in the lining, then threw it back at Adriaen. "Follow me."

Adriaen put his coat back on and tried to gather up a few of the rolls as he followed the man across the small courtyard toward a huge wooden door on the far wall. There the man fumbled with his keys until one of them opened the door. "Down the steps and through the tunnel," he growled. "Tell Ernst that Gunter let you in."

Adriaen stepped into the dark cavern, and the huge door thudded behind him. He heard the key turning in the lock, and a cold chill penetrated his coat. He was inside the dreaded Antwerp prison. He stood still for several moments, waiting for his eyes to adjust to the dim light. But it did no good.

There was no light to adjust to.

Chapter 5

Dungeons and Dragons

EVEN THOUGH ADRIAEN couldn't see, the prison wasn't silent. He knew from the brief glimpse he'd had when the door was open that steps fell away in front of him. He listened to the sounds coming up from below: dripping water . . . a heavy stone being dragged along . . . a scratching sound . . . then from somewhere below came a long, echo-ing moan, almost a wail. Was it a person in pain? Was it his mother? He had to go to her!

He slid a foot forward, reaching out with his hands to find something that would steady him, but his hands found only the damp air. He

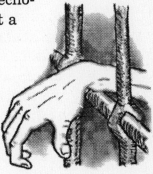

49

took another hesitant step, and his foot dropped over the edge into space. He fell back and landed hard on the slimy stone floor. He was breathing hard, his heart pounding. Unconcerned about the muck under him, he slid forward on his seat, reaching over the edge with his leg.

There, as it should have been, was the next step. He scooted himself down onto it and reached out to find the next step, and then again . . . and again . . . and again. Like a crab, he had worked his way down several steps when suddenly the long, mournful moan echoed again along the tunnel. He hesitated. Was it human? This time it sounded more like an animal howl.

But his mother was in this prison. He couldn't let fear stop him from finding her! He continued to inch his way down the steps. Then he came to a bend; around the corner he could see a dim, flickering light from the bottom of another flight of steps. The light gave him courage; he stood up and continued down the steps, sliding one hand along the stone wall for balance. At the bottom he followed a long passage toward a smoky torch that hung on the wall. The stinking smell of the place made Adriaen gag.

Across from the torch was a small alcove with a bench and a man sleeping on it. The howl sounded again, this time from much closer . . . just down the passage beyond the sleeping guard. The guard stirred at the mournful sound, and Adriaen stepped up and touched his knee. "Are you Ernst?" he asked.

The man jumped to his feet. In the flickering

torchlight, his skin looked yellow and waxy; stringy gray hair stuck out from his partially balding head. The shadow of the wild-looking man danced on the stone wall behind him. "What are you doing in here?" he snapped, dabbing at his right eye with his ragged sleeve. And then Adriaen saw that there was no eyeball in that socket . . . just wet tears running down his cheek.

Finally Adriaen found his voice. "I want . . . I want to see a prisoner," he stammered.

"You want to see a prisoner, do you now? And who might you be?"

"Just a visitor. Gunter let me in."

"I imagine he did," the man sneered. "Think this is a circus or something?"

"No. I've just come to visit someone . . . please."

"Well, then," grunted the jailer with an evil glint in his one good eye, "come with me." He grabbed the torch from the wall and headed down the corridor.

After a short distance he came to a door and turned to Adriaen. "We got us one of them heretics in here. They're a stubborn lot. Sometimes there ain't nothin' that'll make them deny their strange beliefs. But . . . the court says we gotta try—have to give 'em a chance to recant their heresy. So, this one's gettin' his chance. I call this my 'dragon' in here."

The guard swung open the door and entered the large room. Three high, barred windows along the far wall let in a dim light. Huge beams held up the ceiling, and in the center from one of the beams, a man hung by ropes attached to his wrists. He dangled

about two feet off the floor, but another rope attached a heavy iron weight to his ankles. Adriaen

could see that the weight nearly pulled the man in two.

"Now you see why I call it my 'dragon'?" laughed the jailer, waving his torch toward the prisoner. "It's draggin' him in two—heh, heh. *Draggin'* him apart . . . get it?" And he roared with evil laughter as he walked over and put his foot on the weight to add extra pull.

The man screamed out in pain, and Adriaen realized that this had been the wail he had heard as he was coming down the dungeon steps. The scene made his stomach churn and he threw up before he got out of the room.

"Ain't that what you wanted to see?" laughed the jailer as he followed Adriaen out.

"No." Adriaen was almost too afraid to ask to see his mother for fear that she would be undergoing some awful torture, too. But finally he worked up the courage. "You—you got any women down here? There's someone in particular I came to visit."

"And who might that be?" sang the jailer in a whiny voice.

"Just someone I know."

"All right. Come with me." He led the way on down the passage. The end was blocked off with iron bars with a gate in the middle. The jailer lit another torch on the wall near the gate and handed it to Adriaen. Then he unlocked the gate. "On your right we got the women's cells. On your left are the men's. Down at the end we keep the crazies."

Adriaen could see that the end of the corridor was

barred off; beyond it was what looked like a huge cage with dim shapes moving around in it. A single shaft of smoky light slanted in from a high window.

"Don't get near them," the guard cautioned. "They're just like wild animals and could tear you apart. Otherwise, visit anybody you want. When you're done, come back here and call for me . . . if I'm still here, maybe I'll let you out. Heh, heh, heh." He laughed again as he wiped a tear from his eyeless cheek and locked the gate behind Adriaen.

Adriaen moved cautiously to the first door on the right. Bars covered a one-square-foot window in the heavy oak door. He peeked in. The cell was small, maybe eight by ten feet. Down from a shaft at the far side there filtered a dim light, so dim that rather than light the darkness, it emphasized how far away freedom was.

In the gloom, Adriaen could see a couple figures huddled in the corner. "Mama? Mama?" he ventured softly.

The forms moved . . . then one jumped up and ran screaming toward the door. "No! Nooo! No!" the woman wailed as she pounded on the door with her fists.

Adriaen jumped back.

"They didn't get you, too, did they, son?"

Another figure was struggling to shove the first woman away from the window, but in the torchlight Adriaen could see that neither one was his mother. He stumbled away from the cell, horror stricken. If these women weren't considered crazy, how bad did they have to get before they were put into the cage at the end?

He forced himself to the next cell, but by this time the commotion had aroused several of the prisoners on both sides of the corridor, and men and women were reaching their grimy arms through the cell door windows. But Adriaen kept his eyes fixed on the cells on the right, looking at the frightened faces behind the bars.

No one was clamoring at the window of the fourth cell on the right. Adriaen approached it cautiously and peered in. "Mother?" he called softly to the forms sitting against the far wall.

The forms rose slowly and one came forward. "Adriaen? Adriaen? Is that you?" And then his mother was at the bars, crying softly as she reached through to hold his hands. The other three women in the cell—Janneken Munstdorp and two women named Mariken and Lijsken—gathered around her. "Why are you here? How did you get in?"

For several minutes questions flew, each woman wanting news of her own family. "I don't know where they've taken Hans," said Janneken Munstdorp tearfully. She had been married to Hans Munstdorp only a short time before they were captured. "He doesn't seem to be in any of the cells across the way. Have you heard anything about him?"

Adriaen shook his head, wishing he had news. But he could hardly concentrate. "Oh, Mama," he whispered, "how have they treated you?"

To his relief, his mother assured him that they

hadn't been tortured—at least not yet—but each one had been taken out, questioned and threatened. So far, she said, God had given them the strength to not reveal the names of any other believers. But they still hadn't heard about a trial date.

"We are well, Adriaen," she said, patting his hand.

"But the food is terrible," Mariken complained, "and there is not enough of it."

The sack of bread that Adriaen brought wouldn't go through the bars, so he passed in one roll at a time. When prisoners from other cells saw what he was delivering, they began to yell and demand bread for themselves. Adriaen felt guilty, but there was not enough.

When Adriaen explained why no one else had come to visit, his mother said, "Then you shouldn't have come either! What if you are identified and followed home?"

"But I didn't tell anyone who I came to visit. So no one knows."

"I'm afraid it's not that simple," said his mother sadly. "They could figure it out. We are the last women that were put in here. You haven't visited before, so it's logical that you are here to visit us. I don't think your secret is safe, my son."

A chill went down Adriaen's spine, and he looked back down the corridor to see if the one-eyed guard was watching, but he was not to be seen.

"Look," said his mother, "there's only one safe way to get word in and out of the prison. There's a woman named Emma who comes—"

"Yeah, I know her," interrupted Adriaen. "She helped me get in."

"Good. She comes here almost every day to visit her husband. If you paid her a little something for her trouble, I think she would carry messages back and forth between each of us and our families. But the church is right. None of you can come here again! It's too dangerous for everyone."

"But, Mama, that woman, Emma, said her husband is going to be hung a week from Friday. After that she won't be coming anymore."

"Oh . . . well, we'll just have to do the best that we can. She can take a couple messages before then. The first thing you have to get in to us is paper and quill pens and a bottle of ink—"

"And candles," spoke up one of the other women.

"Send food, too, when you can."

"But we can't have too much coming in and out," cautioned Maeyken Wens.

"That's right," said Adriaen. "Gunter checks everything."

"He may be looking for a bribe," said Maeyken. "Whoever makes contact with Emma should have a little extra money available.

"Oh, Adriaen, it's so good to see you. That's the hardest thing for us—to be away from our families. But the Lord sustains us with prayer and singing, and we quote Scriptures to one another. Memorize your verses, son—you can never tell when you will need them."

Maeyken pulled Adriaen close and kissed him

through the bars. For once, he didn't mind it, not even that others were watching or the coldness of the bars on his cheeks.

"You better go now, son. Let's not give them extra time to be figuring out who you are and why you're here." His mother broke into tears, sobbing quietly. "I love you, but . . . don't come back, Adriaen. Don't come back." Then she turned back to the gloom of the cell.

The other women quickly urged Adriaen to greet their families for them and to be alert for any information about Hans Munstdorp. "Be careful," they whispered as Adriaen backed away from the cell, the torch in his left hand flickering on their sorrowful faces.

Chapter 6

The Man in the Burgundy Cloak

WHEN ADRIAEN GOT TO THE END of the corridor, he called out to the guard, "I'm done now." But there was no response. Adriaen rattled the gate. "Guard! Mr. Ernst . . . I'm ready to go now. Please unlock the gate and let me out."

Then he yelled and shook the gate with all his might. "Hey, wake up down there! I want out!" A panic washed over Adriaen, and he felt the fear of being trapped forever in a dungeon. *Get control,* he told himself. *He can't keep me in here. He's probably trying to scare me.*

He waited. The guard had tried to scare him earlier by showing him the man hanging with the weight on his feet. *He's just trying to scare me again, but I'm not going to give him the satisfaction.* Adriaen decided to wait the man out.

Time passed, but nothing moved in the little alcove across from the torch on the wall. The torch was burning low; soon the guard would have to light a new one from the pile of replacements on the floor. Then he would have to show himself, and his foolish games would be over.

Adriaen's own torch was burning down. The part of the straw that had been soaked in oil was just about consumed. When that was gone, the raw straw handle wouldn't last long. But on the floor, just beyond the gate, was another torch only partially burnt. Adriaen stretched his arm through the bars. The torch was a few inches beyond his reach.

He hurriedly looked around for a stick or something to extend his reach. He saw nothing at hand, so he walked back down the corridor, past the cell that held his mother, all the way to the end, outside the cage for the insane people. Still he couldn't find anything. Back at the gate he tried reaching through with his burning torch, but—even though it was long enough—the end of it was too flimsy to catch the other torch and pull it toward him. Using his torch as a tool to drag the fresh torch closer nearly put out the flame. That would have meant big problems.

His eye caught movement beyond the gate. It was something far down the tunnel. Was Ernst returning? Then, as the flame from the far torch died to a smoky, orange glow, Adriaen saw that the movement came from a huge rat scampering along the tunnel.

Maybe he's not there, the boy thought. *Maybe he's left me down here.* "Ernst! ERNST! Open up!" Adriaen screamed, but there was no response.

His own torch was burning lower. Soon he would be in total darkness . . . except for the feeble light that filtered through the cell door windows and from the cage at the end. He reached through the bars again and stretched as far as possible, bruising his shoulder with the effort to shove his arm through the gap just an inch or two farther.

It was no use.

Then he had an idea. He turned around and put his leg through. By twisting and turning it, he forced his knee through the bars, aware that if his knee swelled up at all, he might not be able to pull it back through. The muscles in his thigh compressed, so he kept pushing his leg farther. Finally, as he stretched out the toe of his shoe, it caught on the end of the new torch, and he rolled it closer. He tapped it once again and knew it was within arm's reach.

Now all I have to do is get my leg out, he thought as he pulled it to the knee and began to twist his body. He was in such a strange contortion—having to cling to the bars with his hands to keep his balance—that he dropped his lit torch. It hit the floor, creating a shower of sparks and extinguishing the flame. The dungeon descended into darkness.

With a heave that shot pain up his leg, Adriaen yanked his knee free and dropped to the floor beside the glowing embers of his torch. Carefully he blew on the dull coals until they glowed brightly. Then he stopped, but no flame sprang up. He tried again and again until, to his great relief, a small flame caught. He held the torch upside down until the fire spread.

Once it was burning strongly, he reached through the bars and retrieved the second torch.

He sighed with relief. He would have light for another hour or so.

Certainly, Ernst would return by then. Adriaen was shaking so badly from the ordeal that he sat down to recover while he waited. He let the first torch burn nearly out before lighting the second one.

Adriaen did not know how long he had been staring into the flame when he heard something from down the corridor beyond the gate. This time he was certain. Someone was definitely coming down the stairs. He strained to see, but since he had been looking into the light, it took a few moments for his eyes to readjust. Then he saw a dim glow bobbing on the wall and floor far down the tunnel.

The glow grew brighter until Ernst stepped into the tunnel carrying a torch and called out, "Hey! Who put out my light?"

With his own torch in hand, Adriaen jumped up and called out hopefully, "It went out on its own a little while ago, sir. But . . . I'm ready to leave now."

The one-eyed guard took his time coming to the gate, then he just stood there looking curiously at

Adriaen. "Hey, boy," he said, "where did you get a fresh torch?" Now Adriaen knew that the man had stayed away on purpose hoping the torches would burn out and leave him in the dark. Obviously he knew how long a torch would last, and he had timed his return well after Adriaen would have been caught in the dark.

He's a mean one, but I fooled him, thought Adriaen. *I'm not going to give him the satisfaction of knowing how scared I was.*

"Come on, boy," the guard said with a scowl on his face as he fumbled with his keys. "You can tell me where you got that torch."

Casually Adriaen said, "It was lying right here by the gate."

The guard snorted. "That figures. I sure didn't think that heretic Munstdorp got down off the 'dragon' and came out here to give you one."

Adriaen felt as if he had been struck in the face. That man . . . the one hanging in the first room . . . the one who had been moaning in pain earlier . . . was Hans Munstdorp. He was being tortured.

Adriaen grabbed the bars and shook the gate. "Let me out of here, right now!" he screamed. "Come on, I've got to get outta here!"

"What's the matter?" laughed the guard. "You about to fill your pants or something?" He slowly opened the gate.

Adriaen jumped through and ran down the tunnel.

"Hey, what about my torch?" the guard called after him.

"I'll leave it at the top of the steps," Adriaen yelled without looking back. Once around the corner, he took the steps two at a time and was nearly to the top before he remembered that Gunter had locked that door from the outside when Adriaen had entered the dungeon. There would be more problems getting out!

But at the top of the steps, Adriaen found—with the aid of his torch—that there was a rope hanging through a hole in the ceiling. He pulled on it and could hear a bell ring somewhere outside. He pulled again and again and again.

Suddenly, from outside he heard Gunter call, "Hold your horses. You needn't be in such a hurry." Then a very small window opened in the door, and Gunter said, "Show your face."

Adriaen got close enough to the window for the guard to see who he was, and soon the door swung open.

It was foggy and drizzly in the prison courtyard, but Adriaen had never been so glad to see the light of day. He stepped out and squinted even though the stormy weather made the day rather dark.

"Have a good visit?" the guard asked.

"Sure . . . if any time spent in a prison can be called 'good,'" said Adriaen sarcastically, trying to keep the guard from noticing how scared he was.

Gunter's laugh came from deep within his huge body as he led Adriaen across the yard to the outside gate. "You be sure and come back real soon now. Maybe next time you can stay a little longer," he said with a grin as he let Adriaen out the gate.

✧ ✧ ✧ ✧

Adriaen was halfway home when he had the sense that he was being followed. There were several people on the streets at that time of the afternoon, going about their business and finishing their errands, so it wasn't as though he expected to be alone, but he still glanced back over his shoulder from time to time.

It was when he turned a corner onto Glazer Street and looked back the way he had come that he first noticed the tall, thin man in the long, flowing, burgundy cloak. The man was walking swiftly along the street half a block back, stretching his neck to look past other people—looking in Adriaen's direction. Suddenly he stopped, turned, and began looking into a shop window. It was too far away to be sure, but Adriaen thought that the man was still trying to watch him out of the corner of his eye.

It was the sudden stop that troubled Adriaen most. If the man had been walking along casually, looking this way and that, then stopping to look in a shop window would have been a natural thing. But the man had been walking fast, looking far ahead— *maybe at me,* thought Adriaen. Whipping to a stop to study a shop window when Adriaen looked back seemed unnatural.

On the other hand, Adriaen tried to reassure himself, *something in the window might have caught his eye. Besides, why would anyone be following me?*

But the possible answers that sprang to his mind were not reassuring. His mother was in prison, charged with heresy. The officials were trying to catch other Anabaptists in the city. He had gone to visit her and thereby identified himself with her.

Adriaen darted around the corner and ran as fast as he could past the shops of several glass glazers until he came to an alley. There he turned left— away from his home—and ran to the end. He came out on another street and ran to the next corner, then continued one more block as fast as he could go. Rounding the corner he skidded to a stop, winded. Planted on the corner were some ragged bushes, just the thing Adriaen needed to hide behind. He ducked behind the bushes, then peeked through them and watched where he had come from.

His breathing had almost returned to normal, and he was about to dismiss the whole thing as a foolish panic, when the man in the burgundy cloak came jogging out of the alley looking both ways. Adriaen was about to take off running again when the man seemed to make a decision and started off in the opposite direction.

Adriaen let out a long, slow breath. For the time being, he had given the man the slip. He headed for home, keeping a close watch behind him, but he decided not to run. If the man came this way asking questions, it was more likely that someone would remember a running boy than one just ambling home.

✧ ✧ ✧

Even though he did not run anymore, Adriaen's

heart was still pounding hard when he burst into the apartment at the top of the stairs. But what he saw seemed to suck the breath right out of him.

His father was home. John Metser was there, as well as a third man—a tall stranger . . . in a burgundy cloak. Adriaen gulped and looked back and forth between the men.

"Where have you been?" his father said sternly.

Were they all under arrest? Adriaen studied the stranger's face. The deep lines and wrinkles in his face gave him the appearance of concern rather than anger. His large eyes were clear and penetrating, but they did not appear cruel. He wore a tight skull cap that mostly covered the wisps of gray hair on the top of his head. His beard was full and curly but also gray. He was definitely older . . . *too old to have been chasing me so fast and beaten me here*, Adriaen thought. But he knew that he might be wrong.

"Adriaen?"

"Sorry, Father. I was . . ." *I'd better tell the truth*, he thought. ". . . I went to visit Mama."

"You *what?*"

"I went to visit Mama. Somebody had to," he added quickly.

"Did anyone see you?"

"What do you mean?"

Adriaen glanced at the stranger. A sad, worried expression washed over the man's face.

"Adriaen. Listen to me—it's important," said his father. "Did anyone see you going to or coming from the prison?"

"Of course they did," injected John Metser. "You can't go and come as you please in and out of the prison. The guards have to let you in and out. So the officials obviously know he was there."

"But I didn't tell them who I was," said Adriaen.

"It's not that hard to figure out who you are if you asked to see Maeyken," said his father. "All they'd have to do is guess."

Then the stranger spoke. "Listen, son. Did anything happen during or after your visit that . . . that seemed like they may have been taking special note of you?"

Adriaen looked anxiously at his father. "Who—?"

"Oh . . . please excuse me," said Mattheus. "Brother Simons, this is my son, Adriaen. I hope he has not brought danger on the believers." Then he turned to Adriaen. "Adriaen, this is Menno Simons. He has come to Antwerp to encourage us in this time of persecution."

Adriaen's eyes widened. Menno Simons—the man whose life and writings had helped create the secret churches—here in their own house.

The church leader smiled and extended his hand to Adriaen. As they shook hands, Brother Simons repeated his question. "Did anything unusual happen?"

Adriaen felt awful. He didn't mean to betray the church members, but . . . he wasn't sorry he had seen his mother. Still . . . he'd better tell them about the man who tried to follow him home. "At first I thought you might be the same man," said Adriaen to Menno

69

Simons. "He was tall like you and wore a burgundy cloak."

Menno Simons looked down at his cloak. "It is a rather unusual color . . . but I can assure you that I was not chasing you around the city streets."

Simons looked at the other two men. "I'm afraid, brothers, that we must assume that the authorities have identified young Adriaen, here. Whether or not they followed him successfully enough to discover where he lives, we don't know. But . . . these are dangerous times. We must all take every precaution."

Chapter 7

Life Is Unfair

THE "PRECAUTIONS" ADRIAEN was required to observe during the following days were to remain in the house and not show his face at the windows under any circumstances.

"I will have Betty come over and visit you from time to time," said John Metser. "Since she's the only other young person your age in the fellowship, she may be of some comfort to you."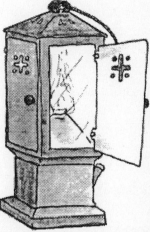

But her first visit the next day was not very comforting to Adriaen.

"Have you heard the news?"

she asked shortly after she arrived.

"What news?" asked Adriaen.

"Some government officials are circulating hand-bills about you. I've seen one. It asks whether anyone knows the whereabouts of a boy running down Glazer Street yesterday afternoon. And then there is a description of you."

A chill went through Adriaen, but he tried to shrug it off. "Maybe they're lookin' for someone else."

"Possibly," Betty said as she started braiding Levina's long, straw-colored hair. "I suppose the description might fit a lot of boys, but think about it, Adriaen. *You* were the one running down Glazer Street at that time. They're lookin' for you. No question about it!"

The same panic Adriaen had felt in the prison when his torch fell to the floor and was snuffed out gripped him with icy fingers. *Had* someone recognized him? Would they report him? Would the authorities come knocking on the door to arrest his father? If so, what would happen to Hans and his sisters? It was all too horrible to think about.

"I thought God was supposed to take care of us," Adriaen grumbled. "What have I ever done to deserve losing my mother? It's not fair."

"Adriaen, don't confuse God with life. Life may be unfair . . . God is not. It wasn't God who put your mother in prison."

"Maybe not, but He didn't stop those men from doing it."

"And you think He should have? You think He

should have stopped the authorities from arresting those believers?"

"Yeah. Why not?"

"Well, God can do whatever He pleases, but when was the last time He stopped *you* from doing something wrong?"

"I don't know," Adriaen said with a shrug, not sure he liked the direction the conversation was going.

"The reason you don't remember is because He very rarely does something like that," said Betty matter-of-factly. "We'd like God to stop *other* people from doing bad things all the time, but when it comes to us, we want the freedom to make our own choices even if they are wrong."

Why did Betty have to sound so . . . so grown up and pious? "Well, it still doesn't seem fair," he muttered, trying to look out the window without getting close enough to it for anyone to look in and see him.

Betty glanced at him out of the corner of her eye as she finished braiding Levina's hair and tied it with a piece of yarn. Tears had come to her eyes and there was a catch in her voice when she quietly added, "When we think about fair, we often count what we lack and forget what we have."

Adriaen kept looking out the window as though he hadn't heard her, but he had. He knew she was referring to the fact that she had no parents—and never had—while he had enjoyed fifteen years with both a mother and father.

She was right, of course. He knew that. He had

many things to be thankful for, but . . . somehow it didn't ease the pain eating away his insides or help him accept the fact that his mother was locked up in that stinking rathole of a prison.

❖ ❖ ❖ ❖

That night all the adults and some of the children from the secret church of Antwerp gathered in the old barn south of town. The weather had turned too nasty to have a worship meeting in a boat on the water again. So they had waited until dark and then come to the barn one or two at a time from different directions so as not to attract attention.

There was only one small lantern in the barn, and it was shielded on two sides so that no light could be seen through the cracks between the boards or when the door was opened. There were benches for the adults, but most of the children sat on the hay. Adriaen felt glad to find an old wooden bucket that he turned upside down for a seat.

"We'll not be doing any singing tonight," John Metser announced. "We can't take a chance on someone hearing us."

Then he introduced Menno Simons and asked if he would say a few words. Menno Simons stood up, and someone adjusted the lantern so that its dim ray of light fell on the old man's wrinkled face.

"I want to tell you how God called me," he began. "I was ordained as a priest in March of 1524 and first served in the village of Pingjum and then in my old

home village of Witmarsum.

"During those years as a priest, most people probably thought of me as a good priest. I did all my duties and preached my sermons, but I did not take my responsibilities very seriously. Instead of studying, I spent whatever time I could playing cards, drinking, and wasting time with other priests.

"Maybe that foolishness was my way of dealing with the doubts I had about the teachings of the state church. The thing that troubled me most was the possibility that the church might be wrong, because such doubts were risky. The church taught that anyone who rejected its teachings would go to hell. But something inside me wanted to know what was the truth, so I went to the Bible—fortunately, I was able to read. There I found that the New Testament clearly disagreed with certain teachings of the state church. So then I faced a choice: Who would I follow—the church or the Holy Scriptures?

"Sometime later, I came across the writings of Martin Luther, who assured me that disobeying the commands of men would never lead to eternal death. As Acts 5:29 says, 'Then Peter and the other apostles answered and said, We ought to obey God rather than men.'"

Menno Simons went on with his sermon, but Adriaen stopped listening. He was thinking about his mother and the other women and Hans Munstdorp. This was a family gathering, but they weren't there with their families.

Suddenly, Adriaen remembered the plan they

had made when he visited his mother in prison—the plan for that woman, Emma, to carry messages in and out for the captives. How could he have forgotten! It was so important . . . and now two days had gone by. Mama probably thought he had forgotten. He *had* forgotten! It was terrible.

Everything had been so confused—getting followed by the man in the burgundy cloak, having to stay in the apartment, Menno Simons coming. But there was no excuse. He had let his mother down . . . in her time of greatest need.

As soon as Menno Simons stopped speaking, Adriaen raised his hand, but in the dark of the old barn, no one saw him. John Metser stood up and was about to speak when Adriaen said, "Brother Metser! I've got something important to say—something I forgot to tell everyone when I came back from the prison."

Adriaen knew it was unusual for a young person to speak up in the meetings, and yet they were family gatherings where children were very important. And Betty had spoken when she decided to be baptized.

"Do go ahead," said Brother Metser, as eager as everyone else to hear anything more from those in prison.

"Most of you have probably heard that I visited my mother and the others in prison," Adriaen began, feeling awkward as all eyes turned on him. "I—I know I can't return to them, but there *is* a way to get messages back and forth."

Murmurs of interest and concern floated among the group.

"There is a woman—Emma is her name—who visits her husband in the prison almost every day. Mama said she would probably carry messages for us."

The murmuring grew louder. "That's wonderful!" ... "Thanks be to God."

Adriaen mentioned the things the prisoners wanted—candles, paper, ink, quill pens, and food. "But ... there is a problem," he admitted. "Emma's husband is going to be hung next Friday, so we'll soon have to find someone else."

There was much excitement and discussion about who should contact this woman, until John Metser stood up and got everyone's attention. "Possibly this idea of contacting that woman is a good plan, but ... I'm still concerned," he said. Brother Metser was always the person most concerned about the safety of the secret church. "There's one other matter we must discuss. You were brave going to the prison, Adriaen, and it's understandable that you wanted to see your mother, but ... you were recognized, and that creates a problem."

Adriaen squirmed as he sat on the upturned bucket. He knew all too well that he had caused a problem—and besides, he hated having to stay indoors all the time.

"We can't let that ... that one situation endanger the rest of the brotherhood. As far as we know, this Emma, or whatever her name is, might have been the person who turned you in to the authorities. What are we going to do about that?"

It was a possibility no one had considered, especially not Adriaen. After all, how *had* the authorities identified him?

The buzzing resumed as pairs of concerned people discussed this possibility. Finally one woman spoke up. "I heard that the boy is staying in his house, and that seemed good enough, but now . . . I don't know. If they know who he is . . ."

"I agree," said John Metser. "And the boy can't stay hidden forever." Adriaen felt the same way. He was going crazy staying inside all the time. Then Mr. Metser continued, "Also, what would happen if the sheriff's men came to search the house and found him there?"

"Come now," protested Adriaen's father. "We can't cover every possibility. At some point we must leave the whole situation in the Lord's hands. After all, He's really the one who protects us anyway."

Then another man spoke up—the husband of one of the other women in prison. "Let's not forget," he said in a voice that cracked with emotion, "it's a privilege to suffer for Christ. I don't want to lose my dear Lijsken, but . . . if God sees fit to call any one of us to witness for Him, we should not shrink from the occasion."

"Yes, but we don't meet on the street corner giving the authorities a chance to arrest us all," John Metser shot back, his voice rising.

"Brothers and sisters," said Menno Simons as he

stood slowly to his feet, "this is not something to squabble over. Remember what our Lord Jesus told us, 'Behold, I send you forth as sheep in the midst of wolves: be ye therefore wise as serpents, and harmless as doves.' We certainly find ourselves in the midst of wolves. The question is, how do we behave wisely without becoming fearful?

"Now, as for the question of whether this woman Emma reported young Adriaen or not, I don't think it makes any difference. His visit alone was enough for them to figure out that he was related to one of the prisoners—"

"That's right," interrupted Mattheus Wens. "If she could have told them more, they would have already come for him."

Adriaen flushed with gratefulness; his father was defending him.

"Probably," agreed Brother Simons. "However, since I need to leave Antwerp anyway—I'm a wanted man, you know, always on the run—let me be the next one to contact Emma. Before anything can come of it, I will be out of town."

Menno Simons turned and looked directly at Adriaen. "As for your concern that young Adriaen will sooner or later be recognized, I have a suggestion."

Adriaen squirmed as he felt all eyes on him once again. What was the man getting at?

"I'm headed north," Simons said. "I could take the boy with me."

Chapter 8

On the Run With Menno

THE IDEA OF FLEEING TOWN with Menno Simons was the last thing Adriaen Wens wanted to hear that night, and his father wasn't any happier about it than he was.

"I won't break up the family," Matteus said in a husky voice. "We've already lost Maeyken; we cannot sustain more loss."

"I know it seems like another sacrifice," Menno reasoned patiently, "but in the long run, it may save the boy . . . and you."

"I'll take my chances," said Mattheus, crossing his arms and sticking out his chin.

"But you're not the only one to be concerned about," said John

81

Metser. "Every person the authorities arrest brings them that much closer to the rest of us."

"Where's the spirit of Christ in you?" challenged Mattheus, uncrossing his arms and leaning forward on his bench as though he were ready to jump to his feet. "Don't the Scriptures say that when it was time for Jesus to face His trial that—and I quote from Luke 9:51—that 'he steadfastly set his face to go to Jerusalem'? Are we so afraid to face our trial that we cannot take a little risk but must break families apart and run like scared sheep?"

"Well, if you're going to quote the Bible at me," Metser retorted, "Jesus also said, 'It is written, I will smite the shepherd, and the sheep of the flock shall be scattered abroad'—that's from Matthew 26:31. So what's the matter with fleeing when that's the safest thing to do? Even Jesus said it would happen!"

"That was a prophecy about Jesus' crucifixion, not what's happening now," shot back Mattheus.

"Then, how about Luke 21:21?" snapped John Metser. "It says, 'Let them which are in Judea flee to the mountains; and let them which are in the midst of it depart out.' That's about the end times, and certainly with all this persecution, we must be in the end times."

"Brothers, brothers, *please*. Let's calm down," pleaded Menno Simons. "It's not a matter of courage, but wisdom. Brother Mattheus, your family has suffered a great blow with the arrest of your dear Maeyken. And other families here have suffered the same. We do not know whether the ultimate witness will be asked of them, but I don't think we have any reason to question anyone's courage. As the Lord promised Paul, 'My grace is sufficient for thee.' When and if the time comes, God will provide the grace for each one to stand as He sees fit. But we must not provoke attack by our foolishness. I think it would be best if your boy came with me."

"Then maybe the whole family should go," Adriaen's father said sarcastically.

But Menno Simons did not get rattled. He merely noted that it would be harder to get a whole family out of the city unnoticed.

There was a long silence.

"I suppose you are right," Mattheus said finally. "Besides, I could not go off and leave Maeyken. We must stay and stand with her."

"And I will not leave her, either," Adriaen jumped in.

"Son, what do you think your *mother* would want you to do?" Menno asked quietly.

Adriaen looked around at the shadows of the other people in the dark barn, then he looked down at his feet. "I don't know."

"Are you sure? Think again. . . ."

The fact was, Adriaen *did* have a good idea what his mother would say. She would not selfishly insist that Adriaen stay here for her. She would think of the others and what was safest for them. "I guess . . . she'd probably . . ." He muttered something softly under his breath.

"What's that? Speak up, lad," said Menno.

"I *said*, she'd probably say I should go."

Mattheus looked quickly at his son, then slowly lowered his eyes.

"Well, then," said John Metser, "I guess that settles it. Now, I think it's time for all of us to go home."

✧ ✧ ✧

The next morning, the Wens household was up before the sun. Elsie was cooking a pot of mush while Adriaen gathered a few of his clothes and put them in a bag. His father was counting the family's money and doing some figuring with a quill pen and a scrap of paper. No one was in a good mood.

"You could just renounce these dumb Anabaptists," ventured Adriaen. "Then you wouldn't have to send me away!"

His father did not respond, but Adriaen noticed the frown on his forehead grow deeper.

"How come I have to go?" Adriaen growled.

"Don't keep pickin' at it, son. You know why. None of us likes the idea—least of all me—but it's been decided. So you must make the best of it. It won't be forever."

His father's instructions had been given in such a tight-jawed way that Adriaen knew he had better not say any more, and yet, he knew his father was on the edge of giving in.

"How come you listen to them and don't make up your own mind, Papa?" he tried again.

His father's fist hit the table, making the coins jingle as he stood up. "That's enough!" he thundered. Then, more quietly as he held out four coins, "Here's half a guilder. Do your best to pay for your own expenses, and be helpful to Brother Menno in every way."

Then Mattheus embraced the boy, holding him to his chest. "I don't want to see you go, son, but it's best. Now . . . Menno Simons will be here in a few minutes, so get some porridge in you."

Even within his father's embrace, Adriaen's arms hung stiffly at his sides. He could not return the hug. He was too upset . . . too angry.

❖ ❖ ❖

Menno Simons and Adriaen were already at the city gates when they opened at dawn. A few farmers were waiting outside to get in, their carts full of buckets of fresh milk, butter, hay, and firewood.

Adriaen's heart lurched when he saw one of the handbills Betty had mentioned nailed to the gate, asking for information about a boy running down Glazer Street on a certain date. He looked around quickly as they walked out of the gate, but no one was paying any attention to them.

They walked mostly in silence through the Belgian countryside all that day, avoiding towns, and that night they stopped at a farmhouse where Menno knew the people. They were welcomed gladly, and the two travelers had no sooner finished eating their soup and bread than several other people arrived, eager to listen to Brother Menno speak.

Adriaen stood in a corner of the crowded kitchen as Menno taught on the meaning of baptism. Adriaen's attention was torn. True, he had been thinking about getting baptized . . . but at that point he was so upset about having to leave home that he didn't want to listen.

"The main disagreement I see between the teachings of the state church and the Scriptures," Menno explained to his eager listeners, "involves how a person is saved. The state church *requires* baptism for salvation and therefore baptizes babies to 'ensure' they will go to heaven before the poor little tykes have any understanding. But Romans 10:9 says, 'If thou shalt confess with thy mouth the Lord Jesus, and shalt believe in thine heart that God hath raised him from the dead, thou shalt be saved.'

"Those are not the responses of an infant. You have to be old enough to understand who Jesus is and accept Him with your own free will. Baptism, then, rightfully comes after a confession of faith as a sign of what has happened in the heart."

Adriaen inched toward the door and slipped out into the night air. There were signs of spring everywhere, but the nights were still cold. He looked south toward Antwerp. *If I left right now, I could be home by noon tomorrow*, he thought. But his feet were tired and sore . . . it would be better to sleep in someone's barn and travel when he was rested.

Then he remembered the handbill posted on the

town gate. Like it or not, he was "wanted," too. *Besides*, he thought, *what would I say to Papa if I came back?*

Even though he was standing in an open farm-yard, Adriaen felt trapped.

He could hear the voice of Menno Simons droning on inside the house. *He's the one who started all this trouble*, thought Adriaen bitterly. *If he had just stayed a regular priest rather than going around the country encouraging people to become heretics, no one would be mad at us. Mama wouldn't be in prison, and I wouldn't be on the run with Menno. A boy shouldn't have to flee his own home.*

"Heretics," he said out loud. The name had a nasty sound to it. "Anabaptists" wasn't much better.

The meeting was breaking up and people were coming outside to return home to their own farms. That night Adriaen and Menno Simons slept in an attic room. The air was cold and there were no windows, but they were each given a thick, goose-down comforter to roll up in. Adriaen was as warm as he'd ever want to be.

❖ ❖ ❖ ❖

The next morning Menno pushed north . . . and Adriaen followed along. As the week progressed, he began to relax around Menno Simons a little more. The old pastor often tried to talk to the boy in a friendly way, and a fellow can only keep a tight lip for so long.

"You know," started Menno one day as they trudged
along a back road, "I was forced to flee my home, too."

88

"How come?" asked Adriaen, curious in spite of himself, even though he wasn't sure he wanted to get into a conversation.

"Same as you: to avoid bringing persecution to my family."

"What do you mean?"

"Well, the authorities are always looking for me because I am fairly well known among the so-called Anabaptists. I can never stay in one place too long. If I stayed around home too long, they would soon identify my family and arrest them as a way to get at me."

"Would they torture them?" asked Adriaen, thinking of Hans Munstdorp hanging in agony from Ernst's "dragon" in the dungeon.

"They might. I wouldn't want to take that chance."

Adriaen didn't want to seem too interested, but he had a question—one that seemed too important not to ask. "How come the state thinks Anabaptists are so bad that they have to chase us—I mean, chase you?" he corrected himself. He had no intention of identifying himself as one of the Anabaptists. After all, it was these teachings that had brought all this pain into his life.

"Good question," responded Menno Simons eagerly. "The state church says that membership is determined by baptism. If you've been baptized by a priest—even if you were too young to realize it—then you are in the church. If not, you're out. We say that's wrong. Membership in Christ's church is based on an experience of salvation through a personal faith in Christ."

Adriaen didn't want to hear a sermon. "Yeah, I know all that. But so what? Why does the government care?"

"Because the state needs the church to help control the common people. Many people might rebel against the nobility or even the king if all they feared for was their life. But when the church says, 'You'll go to hell, too,' then people are less likely to rebel. They don't want to risk eternal damnation. In exchange, the state helps the church stamp out any teaching different than its own."

"You mean heretics?"

"Well, yes . . . people the state and the church consider to be heretics. Controlling the means of church membership is very important to both the church and the state. When we say their basis of membership is wrong, we threaten the state's control as well as the church's power over people. The government cannot allow this. So . . . we are hunted and persecuted as traitors and enemies of the state even though we have never taken up weapons like the Münsterites did."

"Who are they?"

"The Münsterites? Well, not everyone who disagrees with the state church is right. The Bible must be our rule of faith and life. About ten years ago, there was a group of real heretics who went against the Bible and tried to set up God's kingdom in the city of Münster. But they were as wrong as the state church."

"How?"

"For one thing, they resorted to violence, used the sword to fight their enemies. But Jesus was serious when He warned, 'All they that take the sword shall perish with the sword.' Those Münsterites were wiped out."

"By the state?"

Menno Simons nodded.

"Well, I guess the state is some good, then, isn't it?" said Adriaen.

"The Bible tells us that we are to obey the authorities *unless* they command us to disobey God. Then we must obey God rather than man's laws. Yes, the state does serve a purpose, but that doesn't mean we should rejoice when anyone is killed. I know . . . my own brother got caught up in a group like the Münsterites and was killed for it."

Adriaen had forgotten that he didn't want to get into a big conversation. "Did you start the Anabaptists?"

"No, no . . . not by any means," Menno laughed. "You see, not too many years ago, Conrad Grebel and Felix Manz and a few others in Switzerland began baptizing one another based on their confession of faith. But they weren't the first to practice 'believer's' baptism instead of infant baptism. From what we read in the New Testament, this is how it was done in the early church. Not only do all verses that talk about the nature of conversion require an adultlike understanding, but none of the people baptized in New Testament times are said to have been infants."

His question was answered, and Adriaen didn't want to talk anymore. He walked faster, leaving Menno Simons a short way behind. He had talked too much; Menno would think he was beginning to soften. But the pain was still there; all this tension about who thought what about baptism seemed so irrelevant against the hard facts: his mama was in prison, and Adriaen was many miles away from home against his will.

Every day he considered plans for a way to escape. Of course, Menno wasn't holding him captive, but . . . he was just a boy. Where else could he go? Only Menno knew the people who would safely take in a stranger. If Adriaen ran off on his own, the first question would be, "Who are you? Where are you from?" And that could lead to questions by the authorities.

Like it or not, he was stuck with being on the run with Menno.

Chapter 9

Eyes That See Not

LILIES OF THE VALLEY spread their sweet perfume on the spring breezes that meandered through the grove of trees where the two fugitives lunched on bread and hard cheese. They had turned off the dusty road into the woods. Just inside the tree line, they found a small sunny spot with grass and a couple large boulders that made comfortable backrests. It was good to take the load off their feet.

"Look," said Menno Simons, "there are some strawberries. Must be the first of the year."

Adriaen got up and searched about until he had picked a handful of the tiny berries. Then he came back and shared some of them with the church reformer.

They were in northern Friesland, some 150 miles from Adriaen's home. Most of the countryside was typical lowlands—open fields, meandering canals, and frequent marshes. But occasionally, on slightly higher ground, there were groves of oaks and elms. When the wind came from the west or north, it smelled of the sea. "Soon we'll be on the Baron von Ahlefeldt's lands," said Menno. "The baron hasn't actually agreed to protect Anabaptists, but I think he's sympathetic. At least he hasn't driven us off his estate or betrayed us to the authorities yet."

But Menno Simons had no sooner said these words than Adriaen heard the sound of rapidly approaching horses. "Someone's coming," he said anxiously, looking around for a place to hide.

"Stay put," said Menno. "If we failed to hide in time, we would surely arouse suspicion. I think we're better off here." He stretched out on his burgundy cloak and leaned back against the stone behind him, looking relaxed in the warm sun.

Three horsemen moved quickly up the road. One wore the emperor's crest on the front of his tunic, and the other two had swords at their side. Adriaen hoped that they would ride on past without taking notice of them, but it was not to be. One of the swordsmen pointed into the woods, and the riders pulled their horses to a quick stop. After a brief conversation, they moved single file into the grove, weaving and ducking to avoid the low-hanging tree limbs. They came straight toward Adriaen and Menno.

"Oh, Lord," murmured Menno. "Do not let them
see what sits here before them."

Adriaen felt as if his stomach were about to turn inside out.

"Good day, gentlemen," offered Menno as the riders came to a stop—three abreast—in front of them. "Won't you dismount and take some refreshment with us in this beautiful glade?"

"Don't have time," said the one with the crest on his tunic. "We're chasing heretics—one by the name of Menno Simons, to be exact. Ever hear of him?"

"Well, yes, as a matter of fact I have," said Menno. "Older fellow, isn't he? Gray hair, long beard?"

"That's right."

"Then he must look like a thousand other men around here," said Menno with a chuckle.

The official frowned. It was not a joke he appreciated. "This one's different," he growled.

"Oh, indeed . . . in what way?" asked Menno, sitting up and appearing very interested.

"This fellow's one of those dreaded Anabaptists! I don't know how you could have heard of him without knowing that fact."

"Yes, yes, of course, an Anabaptist. Why, I knew that. How foolish of me to not realize it was that which makes him 'different.'"

"I'm glad you understand," said the official, standing up in his stirrups to stretch. "By the way, you haven't seen any Anabaptists pass by here, have you?" he asked.

Menno stroked his beard and looked thoughtful. "No, no . . . in fact, no one has passed by while we've been sitting here."

"Well, keep a sharp eye. You can't miss 'em. And, we'll let you in on something. There's a big reward for anyone who helps us catch this Menno Simons." The riders turned their horses to leave, but just as the last one ducked to go under the limb of the first tree, he stopped his horse and turned back. He looked long and hard, first at Adriaen and then at Menno. "This is the road to Leewarden, isn't it?" he asked.

"Without a doubt," said Menno. "Just a couple hours on down the road . . . or less for someone with such a fine horse as you have."

The man tipped his hat and followed his comrades.

Adriaen did not take a breath until the clip-clop of the horses' hooves had passed out of earshot. Then he gulped in fresh air so fast that he became dizzy. "How'd that happen?" he gasped.

"I don't know, but I believe it was the Lord."

"But . . . they were looking right at us!"

" 'Having eyes, see ye not? and having ears, hear ye not?' " said Menno looking off toward the road where the emperor's men had gone.

Adriaen wrinkled up his face. "What'd you say?"

"Oh . . . sorry," said Menno, returning his attention to Adriaen. "I was just remembering something Jesus said about the Pharisees. They had rejected the truth so long that even when they saw Jesus' miracles, they didn't recognize Him as the Messiah."

"If God did it, how'd He do it?"

"I don't know . . . maybe God made them see no more than what they expected to see: a couple common travelers sitting by the roadside while they imagined that Anabaptists wear strange clothing or act in strange ways—something to set us apart from ordinary people."

"I—I don't get it."

"Neither do I, but that's not the first time God has controlled human vision."

"You mean . . . this has happened before?"

"Maybe not exactly like this, but the Bible tells about several instances when people didn't see what was there and other times when God enabled humans to see what normally can't be seen. Have you heard the story of Elisha's servant?"

Adriaen shook his head.

"The servant was frightened because they were surrounded by enemy soldiers, but the prophet Elisha said, 'Fear not: for they that be with us are more than they that be with them'—meaning the enemy. Then Elisha prayed, and the Lord opened the servant's eyes, and the servant saw that the mountain was full of horses and chariots of fire with warriors ready to protect God's men. Maybe they were angels."

The two travelers put what was left of their bread back in the bag and rose to go. "By tonight," said Menno, giving Adriaen an encouraging clap on the shoulder, "we should get to Hadewijk's Inn. I have often stayed with her. She's a dear sister . . . I think you will like her."

❖ ❖ ❖ ❖

When Adriaen and Menno Simons got to "Hadewijk's Inn," it differed very little from most of the other farms they had stopped at. The "inn" sat in the middle of open fields, far away from any surrounding farms. "Out in the open is the safest place," Menno had explained. "You can see someone coming long before they get there and hide if need be. Of course, that doesn't work so well at night, but it helps."

Hadewijk had another early-warning system—geese, a whole flock of them. They set up a racket that seemed likely to raise the dead when Adriaen and Menno were still a half-mile away. Hadewijk came out of her kitchen, wiping her hands on her apron. She had to shade her eyes from the late afternoon sun to look down the overgrown lane leading to her thatch-roofed house.

Once she recognized Menno Simons, she waved her arm excitedly and took a stick after the biggest gander, which was making the most racket. The noise subsided some, but the geese continued protesting the arrival of strangers until the squawking birds finally waddled around to the other side of the run-down barn.

While Hadewijk was even older than Menno Simons, she was as spry and active as someone half her age. Adriaen felt at ease just by her kindly looks. Her blue eyes twinkled in a tan face that was distinguished by round rosy cheeks and a pug nose. The wrinkles around her eyes and mouth looked like they came more from smiling than old age. She ran her little farm alone except for the occasional help of her guests.

"If I'd known you'd be coming," she scolded good-naturedly, "I'd have fixed you a fine dinner. But come right in . . . I'll scare up something."

What she "scared up" was boiled potatoes and soft-boiled goose eggs. Adriaen hadn't eaten anything so good since he had last tasted his mother's cooking several weeks before.

"Before you go to bed," Hadewijk said, "let me show you what you should do if the sheriff's men come while you're here." Menno already knew the route, so he did not come when she led Adriaen into the low-ceilinged kitchen. "If you have to escape, pull these shelves out . . . there's a passage behind. Go down the steps and follow the tunnel. It leads to the barn. Go out the other side of the barn and you will find a dry canal bed. If you stay low you can follow it until you get to the woods."

"What would happen if they found this passage?" Adriaen asked.

Hadewijk shrugged. "I would just tell them the truth. The former owners made it so that in the winter they wouldn't have to walk through the snow to get to the barn."

Chapter 10

The Judas Fortune

MENNO SIMONS HAD WARNED Adriaen that guests at Hadewijk's Inn were always expected to help out, so he was not surprised the next morning when Hadewijk asked him if he would go into town to pick up some salt and cloth and a few other things that she couldn't make on the farm.

REWARD
Menno
Simons

100 Gold

The closest town was Leewarden—about six miles away—and while Adriaen was shopping in the market-place, he heard a town crier waving some fliers and shout-ing, "One hundred gold guilders, one hundred gold guilders for Menno Simons."

Adriaen quickly purchased the salt and cloth that Hadewijk had requested, keeping the town crier in sight all the time. When the crier left the marketplace, Adriaen put his purchases in an old sack, ran after the crier and asked for one of the fliers.

"Can you read? I'm not supposed to waste these. They're official—from Emperor Charles the Fifth."

"I can read . . . a little," said Adriaen. "Come on. Let me have one."

The crier shrugged, handed one to Adriaen, and went on shouting, "One hundred guilders . . ."

As Adriaen read the flier, his mind began to spin. It forbade anyone from giving Menno Simons aid or shelter or even reading his books. Then it offered one hundred gold guilders to anyone helping to arrest Menno Simons. But Adriaen's eyes were drawn to something written at the bottom: "Should that person or any of his immediate family have committed a crime, he and his family will be fully pardoned upon the successful arrest of Menno Simons."

Adriaen glanced up to see if anyone was watching him, then he stared again at the flier. "He and his family will be fully pardoned. . . . He and his family will be fully pardoned. . . ." Adriaen read the line over again and again.

Pardon . . . that could mean freedom for his mother and no danger for his father! He could go home! The family could all be together again.

Adriaen's mind raced. It had been a long time since the family had lived in peace. Ever since his parents had gotten involved with the secret church, danger had lurked at their door. He sometimes dreamed of going back to the "good old days" when he was a small boy and everything seemed so safe and simple. Maybe . . . maybe this reward would make that dream come true.

But . . . what would the other secret church members say? They would consider him a traitor, that's what. However, with that much money, who cared what they thought? One hundred guilders would make their family rich! They could move anywhere . . . away from other Anabaptists . . . they could buy property—a real house, not an apartment over a smelly butcher shop on a crowded street—and start a new life where no one would know them.

Adriaen looked up. The town crier was half a block away. Adriaen ran after him. "Hey, mister . . . mister!" he said as he caught up. "Who do I speak to if I have some information about this Menno Simons?"

"You? You think you have information? Get lost, kid. I shouldn't have wasted one of those fliers on you. You don't know what you're talking about."

"But I do . . . I mean, I might. Besides, what's it to you if I do or I don't?"

"Just go on home, kid."

"But wouldn't you get in trouble if I did have information, and you refused to help me report it?"

The town crier looked irritated. "All right, all right. If you've got something to say, go to the city magistrate in the courthouse and tell him. If you're lucky, the imperial herald might still be there. He and a couple of his men arrived in town yesterday and delivered these fliers."

"Thanks," muttered Adriaen as he walked away. Suddenly, the strange experience in the woods the day before flashed through his mind.

"Where you goin'? The courthouse ain't that way . . . it's back there," called the crier, pointing the other way. "Hey, wait a minute, boy . . . where're you from, anyway? You talk kinda funny. You're not from around here, are you?"

Adriaen shuddered as if he had taken a chill. It was uncanny . . . when he'd been with Menno Simons, the two of them had not raised any suspicion. God hadn't even let the emperor's men see who they really were—at least that's what Menno Simons had said—even though the description fit Menno right down to the curly beard. But today, the crier recognized that Adriaen was a stranger in town.

"Hey! Who are you?" the crier demanded again.

"None of your business!" shouted Adriaen, and he took off running. He had to think about this. If he turned Menno Simons in, he could collect one hundred guilders *and* a pardon for his mother. What could be better than that? On the other hand . . . what if he were arrested on the spot?

After running a couple blocks, Adriaen slowed to a walk, fairly certain that the town crier was not following him. He sat down on an empty barrel in front of Von Bremmer's Tavern to consider his options. If he went back to the courthouse and the emperor's men were still there, they might recognize him. That could mean trouble—though what kind of trouble, Adriaen wasn't sure.

But if he went on to Hadewijk's Inn, it might be several days before she needed something else from town, and by then, who knew whether she would send him to town alone?

He wanted more time to consider his actions . . . but he didn't know if he had more time. Menno Simons might suddenly decide to move on without notice. He had done that before. "Why tempt the enemy by sticking around too long?" he had explained to Adriaen one Sunday morning on their journey.

Adriaen had not wanted to get up so early. "Don't these people expect you to preach to them today?" he'd asked.

"I suppose they do, but so might our enemies. This will be safer for this little church . . . and for us, too. Sometime I'll be back this way, and I can preach to them then."

No, Menno Simons was too unpredictable. If Adriaen was going to speak to the magistrate of Leewarden, he didn't have much time. Hadewijk would be expecting him back at the inn before long, and if he were late, she would want to know why.

He couldn't give up a chance to win a pardon for his mother. It was now or never. Jumping off the barrel, he headed back toward the courthouse. It was easy to find—other than the tall spire on the state church, the courthouse was the tallest building in the city and could be seen from many points.

Maybe I can find out whether the emperor's men

are there before I go in, he decided. *If they are gone, no one will recognize me.*

At the courthouse, Adriaen was in luck. A beggar sitting on the steps told him that the emperor's "fancy men" had left that morning. "I might be able to tell you where they went if you can spare a coin."

"Sorry," said Adriaen as he ran up the courthouse steps. A servant opened the door and almost sent Adriaen away until he held out the flier. "I have information about this man for the magistrate," said Adriaen.

"What is your information?" asked the servant.

"I'll only tell the magistrate."

"I'm not supposed to disturb His Honor unless there's something of significance. Come on, lad, you tell me, and I'll pass it on."

Adriaen wasn't that stupid. Sure, the man would pass it on . . . in his own name, expecting to collect the reward for himself. "No. I'll speak only to the magistrate."

The servant shrugged and opened the door. "Well, it's your neck if this isn't important."

Adriaen followed him down a long hall to a pair of huge wooden doors. The servant knocked.

There was no response.

He knocked again, and finally someone within growled, "Enter."

In a room with more windows than Adriaen had ever seen except in a cathedral sat a thin old man behind a huge desk. Next to him at a little writing table was a scribe with pen and paper.

"What is it?" snapped the magistrate. "I'm very busy dictating letters."

Adriaen was shaking so much that he spoke in a whisper. "I have information about Menno Simons," he said, holding up the flier.

"Yes . . . as does everyone," said the magistrate as he waved his hand up in the air and rolled his eyes. "He travels around the country preaching rebaptism, and for that shocking news, I suppose you would like to collect your hundred guilders."

For a moment, Adriaen was confused. Is that all he would have to say to collect the money? Then he realized that the magistrate was making fun of him. "No. No," said Adriaen. "I have real news. I know where he is right now. I could lead you to him."

"And how do you know all this?" The old man was not impressed.

"I have traveled with him from . . ." Adriaen almost said Antwerp, but he decided that he shouldn't give away more information than was necessary. ". . . from the south," he finished.

The old man's eyebrows went up. "When was this?"

"For the last few weeks."

The magistrate frowned hard at Adriaen. "That's possible. I had heard he was coming north." He pushed his square hat back on his balding head. "The emperor's men said they thought they were on his trail."

The old man stabbed a bony finger in Adriaen's direction. "Are you telling me that he is in Leewarden right now?"

"No. But I know where he is." Adriaen paused, but seeing a skeptical look come over the magistrate's face, he added, "And he's not very far away."

"Well, where? I don't have all day. Either you know, or you don't. Tell me, and I'll send someone to arrest him. But if he's not there, you'll be locked up in jail for wasting the court's precious time."

The memory of Antwerp dungeon was still fresh in Adriaen's mind, and the thought of jail scared him badly, but he had to be careful. He was only doing this to obtain a pardon for his mother . . . and the money . . . but mostly for his mother's freedom. Without it . . .

Adriaen held up the flier. "This says that if I help you catch Menno Simons, anyone in my family will be pardoned. How do I know that will happen? Does it include. . . ? What if that person has been charged with heresy?"

"Of course, of course." The old man waved his hand impatiently. "Now, do you have any useful information or not?"

"But how do I *know*?"

"It's the emperor's word. Besides, the church officials know that finding a Judas within the Anabaptists is the only way they are going to catch this rebaptizer, Menno Simons. And that Judas would obviously need some . . . some protection."

A Judas? Adriaen felt as if he had been slapped. Was it true? Judas had betrayed Jesus for money, and now he was preparing to betray Menno Simons for mon—

No! It wasn't just the money. He was trying to save his mother, his very own, dear mother, locked up in a stinking prison! He didn't want her to be tortured; he didn't want her to die. Certainly this was different!

"Well. . . ?" the magistrate pressed impatiently. "What information can you tell me? Don't waste my time now."

"I—I'll have to think about it," mumbled Adriaen. Something in the old man's manner made Adriaen mistrust him.

"Think about it?!" screamed the old man as he stood up shakily from his chair. It was hard to believe that such a loud cry came from such a frail body. "You should have thought about it before coming in here! You either tell me now or get out."

Oh, God, Adriaen groaned to himself. *Why do You allow such awful situations to happen?* And suddenly the old anger surged through his blood. God wasn't protecting him from this terrible problem. . . . God hadn't prevented his mother from being captured in the first place. What did God care?

All right, thought Adriaen in a rage. *If God won't take care of my mother, then I'll turn in Menno Simons and rescue her myself!*

"I'll send you word the next time he's to preach," he blurted out. "You can arrest him then."

The old man didn't like the plan, but he finally agreed. "But, I'm warning you, boy," he said, shaking a bony finger at Adriaen. "If you don't do as you've promised, *you'll* be the one on your way to prison!"

Chapter 11

An Old Woman's Escape

When Adriaen got back to Hadewijk's Inn, Menno Simons was gone. "A stranger came by this afternoon—just a little while before you returned—and asked him to come baptize someone," Hadewijk explained. "But he won't be gone long. He said he'd return in a few days. So don't worry . . . he didn't leave you with me for good." She grinned and her eyes twinkled, but Adriaen was not amused at the joke.

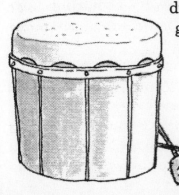

"Come on now . . . it can't be that bad. Look here; I've made you a sweet custard pie. Sit down and try some. You've had a long walk."

A long walk and a lot of bad luck, thought Adriaen as he absentmindedly took a bite of the custard.

"You like it?" asked Hadewijk.

"Yeah, sure." But Adriaen wasn't paying attention. Just when he had a plan, things fell apart. *Or maybe they haven't fallen apart,* he thought. *Maybe I just need to have patience.* He decided that he would go back into town and tell the magistrate what had happened as soon as possible. Maybe that would buy him some more time.

But Hadewijk kept him working for his board and room all day every day, and it was three days before Adriaen got a chance to return to town. Even then he did so by running off when Hadewijk had asked him to dig a ditch in a field far from the house.

When Adriaen told his story, however, the magistrate got very angry and threatened to jail him on the spot. But the boy finally convinced him that he wasn't trying to waste the man's time. "Besides," he reasoned, "if you don't let me go, it will tip off Menno, and he'll likely leave the territory."

"Then I wouldn't have to worry about him anymore, would I? And I could get some of my other work done."

"But—"

"Oh, all right. Get out of my sight, and don't come back until you can deliver that crazy preacher."

That night, back at Hadewijk's Inn, Adriaen was in a sullen mood and didn't notice when the old woman walked up behind him as he was reading the flier for the hundredth time.

"Thinking of solving your problems the quick way?" she asked mildly.

"What business is it of yours?" Adriaen snapped as he jumped up and stuffed the flier into his pocket.

"It won't work," she said calmly.

"What do you mean? How do you know?"

"I mean you can't change God's time. God will protect Menno until the day for him to go Home to glory. You can't make it happen sooner, and no one can keep him here on earth any longer. All you'd do would be to crush your soul with the sin of betrayal."

Adriaen stared at her.

"Sit back down there and let me tell you a story," said Hadewijk. "It happened to me just a few years back, so I can assure you that it's true."

Adriaen sat back down, slumping low in his chair with his arms crossed, glaring at old Hadewijk as she started her story.

"My 'inn,' as it's sometimes called, has not always been out here in the country. I used to live in Leewarden. My husband was the town drummer and played at all the important events, even executions.

"Of course he wasn't needed as a drummer all the time, so he also worked in a glassblower's shop. His best friend on the job was named Snijder. One day the authorities arrested Snijder and sentenced him to death for being an Anabaptist, and my husband was required to play his drum at the execution."

Adriaen started to relax and uncrossed his arms as Hadewijk walked back and forth in the dim lamplight telling her tale.

"Snijder had often told my husband about his beliefs, so he knew him well and did not think his friend was a heretic. In fact, my husband may have been a believer himself. Now, one reason drummers are needed at the execution of heretics is to prevent them from being heard if they try to preach to the crowd. The drummer is sup-

posed to play so loudly that the heretic can't be heard if he tries to preach.

"Well, as you can imagine," said Hadewijk as she pulled a chair around and sat down before Adriaen, "my husband couldn't face the idea of drumming at his best friend's execution, but he had to do it. It was his duty, and if he failed, he, too, would be in trouble.

"So, to ease his pain, he got drunk . . . so drunk that instead of beating the drum, he began to preach what Snijder had told him about the Gospel."

Adriaen smiled at the ironic turn the story had taken. *That would have been something to see,* thought Adriaen, *a drunk drummer standing there preaching to the crowd.*

"That night," continued Hadewijk, "when my husband sobered up and realized what he had done, he decided that his only chance was to flee. So he left town, and . . . I have never seen him since. I missed him terribly. . . ." Her voice trailed off.

"It wasn't long after that that I started taking in traveling strangers—many of them Anabaptists on the run—praying that someone would be equally kind to my man."

Hadewijk sighed and looked around the room. "Can I make you some tea?" she asked.

Adriaen nodded and Hadewijk was up and filling the kettle while she continued to tell her story.

"One day a young woman named Elizabeth came to stay with me. She had been living in a convent where she had learned to read Latin. One day she got ahold of a Latin Bible, and in it she discovered the truth of the Gospel and became converted. She was thrown in prison for a year for her new ideas, and when she got out, she escaped from the convent at her first chance and came to live with me."

Hadewijk returned to her chair and said, "Even back then Menno Simons stayed with me whenever he was in the area. Elizabeth learned much from him and became a well-known Bible teacher for the secret churches in the area.

"Because of her teaching, I was not surprised one stormy night when a heavy knock on my door was followed by three men who barged in and grabbed us. 'We've caught his wife!' bellowed one of them. 'So the heretic can't be far off.' They thought that Elizabeth was Menno Simons' wife. Nothing she said could convince them otherwise, and they dragged us both off to prison.

"Now . . . this is the part of the story I want you to hear," Hadewijk said as she went to pour the tea. When Adriaen had taken his first sip from the steaming mug she handed him, she went on.

"They put us in separate cells and told me that I would be 'examined' the next day—by torture if need be. I was terrified. I was certain that I couldn't stand torture, but I didn't want to deny my Lord or betray other believers by revealing their names."

Adriaen squirmed at the word "betray." He didn't want to be a betrayer, either. But when it came down to his mother or Menno Simons . . .

"Anyway," continued Hadewijk, "knowing that my fear of torture made me weak enough that I might give in, I started praying that God would deliver me. You know, God has promised that He won't allow us to face more than we can tolerate but will always provide us a way to escape. So I asked Him to deliver me from the torture.

"Suddenly, I thought I heard someone calling my name. I looked up, but no one was in my little cell, so I returned to praying. Again I heard my name called, but no one was there. It was a very small, dark cell.

"Then," continued the old woman with a far-off look in her eyes, "the voice came again and said, 'Hadewijk, I tell you, come out.' This time when I looked up, my cell door was open, so I walked out. It was like I was in a dream. Each door opened as I approached it until I found myself out in the street. Then I woke up. How I had gotten out there on the street seemed unreal, but there I was.

"Now . . . what do you make of that?" she asked as she leaned back and squinted at Adriaen.

Adriaen was astonished . . . but he merely shrugged. "I don't know. Maybe you dreamed it."

"Not hardly," she said, shaking her head. "It's a matter of record in the Leewarden courthouse that I was arrested, thrown in prison, and then escaped. Obviously, I'm here today. Poor Elizabeth was tortured severely and then drowned. But the Lord knew that she had the strength for it. She never denied her Lord or betrayed any other believers. So I ask you again . . . what do you make of that?"

Adriaen shrugged. There was that word "betray" again. It reminded him of his deal with the magistrate.

"Come on, boy. You can't get off with just a shrug. Think about it! What happened?"

"Well," said Adriaen, feeling very uncomfortable, "I guess God delivered you."

"That's right. And that's what I was trying to tell you. When Menno's time has come, God will take him. Before then, neither you nor the emperor himself can touch him. God can and will protect him." She stopped and sipped her tea, letting the silence fill the room.

An idea crept into Adriaen's mind. Maybe he could collect the reward and obtain his mother's freedom without anything terrible happening to Menno Simons. If Hadewijk was right, then God could break him out of prison just like He had freed her . . . and the apostle Peter. Adriaen remembered the Bible story his father had told them the Sunday after his mother had been arrested. Maybe turning Menno in wouldn't be so bad. . . .

"Don't even think about it!" warned Hadewijk through clenched teeth. It was as though she had read his mind. "You would only bring damnation on yourself. If your faith has grown enough to believe that God could deliver Menno, then use that faith to believe that God will be with your mother . . . no matter what happens to her."

The boy squirmed under the old woman's gaze.

"You know," she added, "it's an honor to suffer for our Lord after He gave His life to save us. I'm not proud that I was too weak to face it . . . but God had mercy. Don't tempt Him with your own sin."

Chapter 12

Letters From Prison

O NE DAY ABOUT A WEEK LATER, just before noon, Menno Simons returned. Adriaen expected Hadewijk to immediately tell Menno about Adriaen's plans to betray the preacher to the authorities, but if she said anything, Adriaen heard nothing of it.

Instead, when the three of them had finished their first meal together, Menno pulled a packet of letters from his pouch and shuffled through them. "Here," he said. "This might interest you." And without further comment, he handed one of the letters to Adriaen.

Adriaen recognized his mother's handwriting. Hurriedly, he excused himself and went out to

the barn to be alone. Climbing on top of the hay-stack, he opened the letter and began to read slowly.

My dear son, Adriaen,

This may be my last communication to you, so please consider what I say. Because you are my oldest child, I urge you to reverence our dear Lord. You are getting old enough to know what is good and evil—think of Betty, who is about as old as you are.

My son, even in your youth follow what is good, and reject what is evil; do good while you have time. Let your father be your example— how lovingly he went before me with kindness and courteousness, always instructing me with the Word of the Lord.

Hear the instruction of your mother: Hate everything that is loved by the world, and love God's commandment.

Join yourself to those who fear the Lord, depart from evil, and do all that is good with love. Don't look to the world and the ancient customs worldly people follow. Look to the little flock, the church, which is persecuted for the Word of the Lord. The good persecute no one, but they are the ones who are persecuted.

My dear son, yield yourself to that which is good; the Lord will give you understanding.

This may be my last good-bye.

Job 13:15.

Your loving mother, Maeyken Wens.

P.S. Write me a letter as to what your heart says, whether you desire to follow the Lord or not. I should like to know. It would give me great strength to face my trial.

The tears were pouring freely down Adriaen's cheeks by the time he finished the letter. He threw himself back on the hay and sobbed. He cried so hard he thought his insides were tearing apart. He didn't want his mother to die! He didn't want to lose her. He kept remembering when he was a little boy, sitting in her lap while she rocked him . . . why couldn't it be that way again?

After about half an hour of weeping, when he felt as if he had no tears left, he began to think again about saving her. He had a plan that would free her from that awful prison and save her life as well. He was sure it would work . . . and just as sure that nothing else would work. She was locked in that dark, smelly dungeon. There was no other way out.

By now maybe she'd been tortured. Maybe that beast Ernst had used his "dragon" on her . . . or maybe she had been burned with hot irons, or maybe her fingers and feet had been crushed with the hideous screw clamps Adriaen had heard about. His stomach revolted as his mind sorted through the many means of ghastly torture.

But he had a plan!

He pulled the wrinkled, dog-eared flier out of his pocket and stared at the offer to the person who turned in Menno Simons: "Should that person or any of his immediate family have committed a crime, he and his family will be fully pardoned upon the successful arrest of Menno Simons."

Maybe his mother needed a doctor's care. With the one hundred guilders, he could afford the very best. She would recover, and he could sit in her lap again—

No, I'm too big for that, he thought, *but the little ones aren't. God can't blame me for wanting my sisters and brother to have a mother to hold them, especially little Hans.*

The thought of his little brother caused Adriaen to burst out in tears again. A little boy needed his mama. "Even I . . . need a . . . a mother!" he blurted between sobs.

In his pain, anger again stirred within him . . . anger at Menno Simons for spreading this Anabaptist faith, anger at God for letting his mother get captured.

Through blurry eyes he looked again at his mother's letter. How could she tell him to "join yourself to . . . the little flock, the church, which is persecuted for the Word of the Lord"? He knew she meant the Anabaptists. But what they stood for was going to get her killed.

It made him so angry! Why had she believed Menno Simons? Why had she gone to that prayer meeting? Why had she gotten herself arrested? If she would have just remained a quiet, loyal member of the state church, none of this would have happened.

Suddenly he realized he was being angry at his mother, as well as Menno Simons and God . . . and it struck Adriaen that something was very, very wrong with his thinking. How could he be so angry at the person he loved most, his mother?

He looked back at the letter and noticed the line

that said, "The good persecute no one, but they are the ones who are persecuted." He knew that was true . . . obviously true. The Anabaptists weren't persecuting anyone. It was the emperor and the state church—they were the "world" his mother warned against. "Reject what is evil; do good while you have time," his mother had written.

Adriaen looked back and forth at the two sheets of paper that he held in his hands. One was a printed flier from the emperor. The other was a simple note written in his mother's own hand. The first represented the easy, "safe" way; it even promised wealth and protection. The other was the hard way and called him to more suffering and pain. Certainly his mother was suffering . . . but he was suffering, too.

He wanted so much to please his mother. She had even asked him to write and tell her whether he was going to follow the Lord or not. But this decision was too big to base on just pleasing her. It was literally between life and death. She didn't know about the emperor's flier and the chance it offered for pardon and freedom. It was his decision; no one else could make it for him.

As he lay quietly in the hay, Hadewijk's story came back to him. As he thought about it, he began to see that it wasn't a matter of choosing between his mother's wishes and the emperor's offer; it was a choice between whom he trusted—the emperor or God. The emperor's flier told him what would happen if he followed it. But if he followed the Lord there was no promise about the future except that God was powerful enough to free the apostle Peter and even Hadewijk from prison. Adriaen had even glimpsed that supernatural power when the emperor's men didn't recognize Menno Simons that day in the woods.

But was that what happened? Maybe he and Menno had just been lucky . . . maybe God had nothing to do with it. His mind swung wildly between the idea that it was just an accident and the conviction that it had been God's doing. *It makes all the difference*, thought Adriaen to himself. *It's either one way or the other . . . but I can't prove it. I guess that's what faith is, choosing what I'll believe about God! I have to decide whether I'll trust Him . . .*

Adriaen reread his mother's letter once more and noticed at the end, just before her signature, a Bible reference: Job 13:15. What did it say? She was trying to say one more thing to him; maybe it would give him his answer. He had to find out.

He carefully folded the papers and put them back into his pocket. Then, after wiping his eyes and sniffing back the signs of his crying, he headed for the house. Somehow he had to borrow a Bible and find out what was in that verse.

When he came in, Hadewijk was knitting. She held her finger to her lips and whispered, "Brother Simons is very tired after his long journey . . . he's taking a nap." Then she reached out to feel Adriaen's head. "Are you all right?" she worried. "You look a little flushed."

Adriaen swallowed hard so that he wouldn't cry again and said quickly, "Hadewijk, do you think I could have a look at Menno's Bible?"

"Why, I'm sure he wouldn't mind . . . but I still have Elizabeth's old Latin Bible, and she taught me how to read it some. Would you like me to get it?"

Adriaen would have preferred reading the verse himself in his own Flemish language. But if Hadewijk could read Latin, there was only one verse, and she could probably give him the sense. So he agreed.

"Here it is," she said, carefully unwrapping the old text from a small blanket. "What would you like me to read?"

"Job 13:15."

It took Hadewijk several minutes to find the verse, and then she struggled with the Latin words.

"This means 'kill me,' " she explained. "And now this last phrase is, 'I will trust in him' . . . I'm sure of that. But there are a couple other words that don't come to me so easily. Let me work at them a little."

Suddenly her face brightened. "Of course. I should know this verse by heart. . . . 'Though he slay me, yet will I trust in him.' "

"Are you sure that's what it says?" asked Adriaen.

"Yes, yes. That's it. . . . 'Though he slay me, yet will I trust in him.' Martyrs often use it."

"But why? What does it mean?"

"It's a statement of trust, Adriaen. It is the deepest trust one can have in God. It is the trust that, even though we don't understand what is happening to us, we believe that God loves us and will give us the strength to go through even death."

"But why? Why would God allow someone to suffer if He loves the person?"

Hadewijk picked up her knitting. "We may never know the whole answer in this life, but the Bible gives an example that suggests an answer. God loved Jesus, His only Son, and certainly had no desire to see Him suffer. And yet, to accomplish a greater good, He sent Jesus to earth to die in our place. I think the only time God allows us to suffer is when He is allowing us to take part in a plan to accomplish some greater good. Sometimes it's to teach us something—you know, some lessons are hard ones, but we've got to learn them. And sometimes our suffering benefits other people."

"But . . . how could my mother being in prison and maybe even dying help anyone?"

"I don't know, child . . . I truly don't know. The apostle Paul wrote to the Philippians saying that he wanted to take part in what he called 'the fellowship of his sufferings'—meaning Christ's sufferings. He believed it was important. But I can't explain to you what specific good your mother's suffering will accomplish. Maybe someone will someday be inspired to put their faith in Christ because she wouldn't deny her faith. I don't know. I can't prove it to you. It's a question of trust. Can we trust Him . . . come what may . . . or do we try to take matters into our own hands?"

Adriaen closed his eyes. Yes. That was exactly the question.

Chapter 13

A Watery Grave

THAT EVENING MENNO SIMONS was invited to speak at a local prayer meeting. He did not invite Adriaen to go with him or tell him where the meeting would be held. And Adriaen, not having settled the question of which sheet of paper he was going to follow—the emperor's flier or his mother's letter—did not feel like accompanying the old preacher.

The next morning Menno still had not returned. After a breakfast of hot porridge and a cup of tea, Adriaen went outside to cut wood for Hadewijk. He seemed to think most clearly when he was doing hard work.

Earlier that year a spring storm had blown down an old elm tree; now that summer had set in, it was time to make firewood out of it. As Adriaen swung the axe, he remembered something his father used to say: "When you cut your own wood, it warms you twice—once when you cut it and again when you burn it."

But who needs the first warming if you're cutting it in the summer . . . which is usually when you have to gather wood, thought Adriaen as he wiped the sweat from his forehead. Even though it was still morning, the humid air was heating up.

Adriaen surveyed his work and decided to cut off a large limb and drag it into the shade of the barn to cut it up. That would be closer to the woodshed anyway.

But he had no sooner set to work on severing a limb as thick as his leg when Hadewijk's geese set up a terrible racket.

Someone must be coming, he thought. *Probably Menno, returning from his meetings. I've got to hurry and make up my mind. I may not have much time. There's no telling when he might take off for good . . . with or without me.*

The geese continued to honk and scold as Adriaen swung the axe until out of the corner of his eye he saw movement. He looked up and was shocked to see, not Menno Simons, but the emperor's three men—the imperial herald and two swordsmen—the same men he and Menno had met in the woods on their way north. He looked around for a way to escape and was about to run around the side of the barn when one of the men pointed and called out to him. "Hey, you there! Come over here. We want to talk to you."

Adriaen knew running now would be futile. If he took off across the fields, he would be no match for men on horseback. So he walked straight toward them. Maybe once again, God would not allow them to see what was before them.

The imperial herald was the first to speak. "I've seen you before," he said, pointing his finger toward Adriaen.

"Yeah," said one of the other men. "He was with that old man in the woods. Remember? We talked to them the day before we got to Leewarden."

"Is your father here, son?" said the herald.

"No." Adriaen was thinking fast. If there was ever a time to tell them about Menno, this was it.

"We heard that Menno Simons was staying out this way. Remember? We talked to you about him on the road . . . he's that notorious Anabaptist. I hope you've kept your eyes open like we said."

One of the other men leaned over and spoke behind his hat, but Adriaen still heard him mutter, "I think the kid knows more than he's letting on."

"Listen here, young man," said the herald sternly. "This is serious business. If you're withholding information, you could be imprisoned yourself. Have you ever seen inside a prison?"

Adriaen nodded. All the cold, dark misery of the

Antwerp dungeon came back to him in an instant.

"Then you know it's no place to spend a beautiful summer." He waved his arm and looked up at the blue sky. "So think about it before you answer. Then tell me the truth, the exact truth, and nothing but the truth. You understand?"

Again, Adriaen nodded. Terror was pressing inside him, ready to break out like the rising tide against a weak sea dike.

"So I'm asking you: Do you know where Menno Simons is?"

There it was!

But no sooner had the herald put forth his question than Adriaen realized that he still had a choice, a perfect choice. He could honestly say no, because, in truth, he didn't know where Menno had gone the night before or where he was right at that moment. Or . . . he could use this as his opportunity to collect his reward. It would even be safer reporting to the imperial herald. From the beginning he had had a nagging fear that the city magistrate might try to cheat him in some way. But surely the imperial herald would deal honestly with him.

Adriaen looked at the herald. He felt light-headed, and the whole scene seemed to swirl. *Maybe this time I'm the one who's not seeing things as they are. "Having eyes, see ye not? and having ears, hear ye not?"* The words of Jesus buzzed in his mind. He did not want to be one of those people who rejected God so often that he couldn't tell what was right and wrong. He did not want to harden his heart.

"I . . . I don't . . ." he began. Then the opportunity for a pardon—freedom!—for his mother grabbed him; time seemed to stand still as his mind raced. He couldn't let her stay in prison! But . . . a new realization flooded his mind. His mother could get out of prison in a moment, if *she* chose to. All she had to do was deny her faith and her baptism, and the authorities would release her.

But she had not done so! Why?

Why had she resisted the temptation?

Adriaen knew the answer. It was because she trusted God. It all came back to that one question. Could he trust God? *Would* he trust God?

He made up his mind. "No, I don't know! I don't know where he is!" Adriaen said with a set face and a firm jaw.

"He's lying," snapped one of the swordsmen.

"Possibly," said the herald as he started to turn his head toward Hadewijk's house while keeping his squinted eyes focused on Adriaen. "But if he is, he will suffer. . . . Search this place!" he ordered.

He remained mounted on his nervous horse as the other men first chased Hadewijk out of the house and then searched it. The old woman stood in the yard wringing her hands. Her eyes were closed, her lips moving, but she said nothing. Adriaen knew she was praying.

The men searched and searched hard. He could hear things crashing in the house as they tipped them over looking for some evidence of Menno Simons' presence. In spite of the warmth of the noonday sun, Adriaen shook as if he were catching a chill. Menno may have taken his Bible, but there were other things—his burgundy cloak, his writing materials. Adriaen knew they were in the house somewhere. It was only a matter of time before the men found them; then they would know that Menno had been there.

But after half an hour, they came out empty-handed.

"Burn the barn," ordered the herald. "And keep a sharp eye; if Simons comes out, don't let him get away."

"No, no, not my barn," pleaded Hadewijk. "I'm a poor woman. I could never replace it. And my goats, some might be in there. Can't you just search it?"

But the herald paid no attention to her, and soon the fire was blazing in the hot afternoon sun.

The barn burned for a couple hours, but the emperor's men did not find Menno Simons or any evidence of him. Disgruntled, they wheeled their horses and rode off to look for him elsewhere.

With the sour smell of smoke filling the air, Hadewijk sighed. "The goats are safe," she grinned. "Once the fire started, I noticed they were down by the canal."

"But how did they miss Menno's cloak and other things. Did God blind their eyes again?"

"Possibly . . . with a little help from me. I heard the geese and tossed his things into the tunnel while the men were out here in the yard talking to you. It was wise of you to keep them busy so long."

Adriaen knew it hadn't been any wisdom of his own. He had been on the brink of betraying Menno.

But standing there beside what was left of the smoldering barn, he felt a strange peace. He had made his decision . . . to trust God, no matter what.

✧ ✧ ✧ ✧

Menno still hadn't shown up after a couple days, but by now Adriaen realized that the Anabaptist preacher's comings and goings were completely unpredictable—for good reason. But he didn't mind . . . during the long, motherly talks with Hadewijk in the evenings, Adriaen slowly laid down his anger and asked God for forgiveness.

"I want to be baptized," he said after a late-night talk.

Hadewijk beamed. "I see no reason why you shouldn't be baptized. You can ask Menno to baptize you when he returns. There's no charge for the use of my canal," she joked.

But the idea of telling Menno about his decision had been worrying Adriaen. "Do you think I'll have to tell him . . . *everything* that's happened?"

"Confession is part of conversion. The apostle John said, 'If we confess our sins, he is faithful and just to forgive us our sins, and to cleanse us from all unrighteousness.' "

"But, I did tell God that I was sorry when we prayed."

"Yes, and God has forgiven you, but it was also

something between you and Menno. You were on the verge of betraying him to a certain and horrible death. I know Menno won't hold it against you—he's not that kind of person—but *you* may not feel comfortable around him until you speak of it openly. Confession will free you."

❖ ❖ ❖

Menno Simons showed up the next day. The prayer meeting had led to another, and another, and another as the graying preacher went from town to town encouraging the small secret churches.

And Hadewijk was right. Confession did make Adriaen feel better, especially when Menno Simons—after listening quietly—finally said, "Adriaen, you may have thought that your struggle was about my life, but it was really over your soul. God has forgiven you, and I can do no less. I forgive you, too.

"However, there is one thing I should tell you. I would be honored to baptize you, but to do so puts you at greater risk. If the authorities discover that I baptized you, they will make greater effort to force you to recant your faith and betray others . . . as a way of getting back at me.

"For that reason, I have baptized very few people. I let others do the baptizing."

Menno looked calmly at Adriaen, not in any way suggesting what the boy should do.

Adriaen took a deep breath. "I would like you to baptize me," he said.

Menno Simons smiled. "Let it be Sunday, then, in Hadewijk's canal. We will invite a few other believers from the area to witness your commitment and celebrate with us."

✧ ✧ ✧ ✧

That Sunday when Adriaen walked down into the canal beside Menno Simons, he carried in his pocket a small stone and the emperor's flier offering the reward for the arrest of Menno Simons.

When Adriaen was asked to tell about his conversion, he spoke clearly so the little knot of believers on the bank could hear as he told about his faith in Christ and decision to follow Him in an adult way. Then he pulled out the stone and the flier. He told about his anger toward God for letting his mother be captured. Then he read the flier and explained the plan he'd had to betray Menno Simons. "It was my way of getting back at God, I guess. I didn't like how He was handling things, so . . . I was going to take over and do it myself. I was wrong."

His voice caught, and he feared he might cry, but in a moment he continued. "I wish to bury this flier and my anger . . . my anger at God in this watery grave so that when I am raised up I can live a new life in Christ." Then he wrapped the flier tightly around the stone and put his hand below the surface of the water. Then he turned toward Menno Simons.

As the preacher lowered him under the water, Adriaen released the stone weighted flier.

When Adriaen rose from the water, it *was* to a new life in Christ . . . but it was not to a safe life. As he waded to shore where the other believers sang hymns of praise, he knew he joined them as a wanted man.

While everyone was hugging Adriaen and shaking his hand, he noticed that Menno Simons was greeting a man in dirty clothes who looked like he had been traveling a long time. Soon the two approached Adriaen.

"This is Brother John," said Menno. "I think he has some news for you."

"Here," said the stranger as he handed Adriaen a letter. "It's from your mother."

Adriaen quickly opened the small, folded parchment and read.

My dear Adriaen,

I did not know whether I would have another chance to write to you, but I hope this letter reaches you safely.

I have written it after I was sentenced to die at the stake for the testimony of Jesus Christ. Lord willing, my witness will happen on the fifth day of October.

Do not fear this suffering which I must face; it is nothing compared to the suffering which endures forever for those who reject God. The Lord has taken away all my fear; I cannot fully thank Him enough for the great grace He has shown me.

Though I will soon be taken from you, I

pray that you will follow Christ so you will have your mother again in the New Jerusalem where we will never again have to part. Follow me in faith if you value your soul, for there is no other way to salvation.

Love one another all the days of your life. Take little Hans in your arms now and then for me. And if your father should be taken from you, care for one another.

Good-bye once more, my dear Adriaen. Be kind to your father in his distress, and do not cause him any grief.

Your loving mother,

Maeyken Wens

When he had finished the letter, tears were streaming down his face, but he did not care who saw them. "I must go to her," he blurted out to Menno Simons. "She must know that I, too, have chosen to follow Christ. Besides, if she must make her witness, the least I can do is honor her with my presence." He looked back and forth between Menno and the stranger. "It would give her strength."

Menno took a big breath. "Well, son, I guess that's possible now. According to Brother John here, the authorities have identified most of the believers in Antwerp by other means. Whether that will bring more persecution, only the Lord knows, but your presence in the town should no longer create any extra risk to the church there. They have sent word that you can return. However—"

"Then I must leave today!"

"Just a minute. There's something else you must consider. Your return may no longer put others at risk, but, as a baptized believer, you would be in danger yourself."

Adriaen nodded soberly. "I thought about that before I asked to be baptized. That risk exists wherever I go." He held up the letter he'd just received. "I want to have the courage of my mother. If I am asked, I will not deny the Lord just to save my neck."

A smile tugged at the edges of Menno Simons' mouth. "I believe you," he said. "You're not a Judas. You proved that when you chose not to betray me. I trust you, Adriaen Wens." And he reached out and warmly clasped Adriaen's hands in his own.

More About Menno Simons

Menno Simons was born in Witmarsum, Friesland (Northern Netherlands) in 1496. He was ordained as a priest in the Roman Catholic Church in 1524 and served dutifully until he became uncomfortable with some of the traditional teachings, such as infant baptism.

Agreeing with Martin Luther that the Bible was the Christian's highest authority, Menno Simons turned to the New Testament to resolve his questions. From it he concluded that the state church was in error on several important points and left it in 1536 to be rebaptized by Obbe Philips.

Menno Simons was not the founder of the Anabaptists. That distinction falls to Conrad Grabel and his decision to be rebaptized in 1525. However,

Menno was soon asked to become a preacher and leader among the congregations of Anabaptists in northwestern Europe.

One of his early concerns was guiding the new believers away from the Münsterite cult. In 1535, in the town of Münster, a group of revolutionaries left the Catholic Church, also noting many of its errors. But they set up a rebel government intent on taking over the "world" by force.

There was much confusion among the common people in those early years of the Reformation, and the Münsterites were sometimes called Anabaptists. But the Münsterites were very different, and Menno did everything he could to guide new believers away from them.

Far from taking over the world by violence, Menno and most Anabaptists believed in peace and refused to use violence against anyone, even in their own defense. It is for this reason that the story of Dirk Willems and his willingness to give his own life to save that of his captor (who had fallen through the ice while chasing him) became a classic example of Jesus' teaching to return good for evil.

Even today, one of the distinctives of Mennonites and other Anabaptists (which also include the Hutterites, the Amish, and the Church of the Brethren) is their nonviolence, which includes conscientious objection to serving in the military.

However, even though the Anabaptists were not rebels against the state, their rejection of the state church posed a serious threat to both the church and the state. And both institutions conspired to wipe them out.

Persecution was severe for all reformers, but it was most deadly against the Anabaptists. In the town of Antwerp, for instance, where Adriaen Wens's mother was burned at the stake, a total of 248 Anabaptists were executed. No one knows how many Anabaptists were martyred in all of Europe, but conservative estimates are around four thousand. Other historians double or triple this number.

In 1543 the emperor put a price of a hundred gold guilders on Menno Simons' head hoping some greedy follower would betray him to the state. However, by God's grace and heroic help from fellow believers, he was never caught and died a natural death in 1561.

Throughout his ministry, Menno adhered to orthodox Christian beliefs but rejected those that were not mentioned in the New Testament. He believed in the divinity of Christ and baptized only those who asserted their faith in Christ. In his view, military service and killing were wrong, as was the taking of oaths, the holding of the office of magistrate, and marriage to persons outside the church.

Anabaptists, unlike any of the other major Reformation movements, insisted on the separation of church and state. They believed that though church had the right—even duty—to comment on the morality of secular laws, it should not be dictating those laws. In a like manner, they believed that the state should have no part in regulating religion. In so doing, they pioneered with their monumental suffering the concept of religious freedom. In this their influence far exceeds their modest numbers. These principles became the very foundation for democracies such as the United States.

For Further Reading

Bender, Harold S. *Menno Simons' Life and Writings*. Scottdale, Penn.: Mennonite Publishing House, 1936.

Douglas, J.D., and Philip W. Comfort. *Who's Who in Christian History*. Wheaton, Ill.: Tyndale House Publishers, 1992.

Simons, Menno. *The Complete Writings of Menno Simons*. Scottdale, Penn.: Harold Press, 1956.

Vernon, Louise A. *Night Preacher*. Scottdale, Penn.: Herald Press, 1969.